VAMPIRE MA~~STER~~

For Virginia Ironside, writ~~ing~~ a complete release from the page editor. "You can write ~~wouldn't~~ ever condone on the ~~sy you can~~ be as naughty as yo~~~~ and horrible things happening and ~~~~, that's great."

Vampire Master isn't just ab~~out vampires~~, it's about a school too – Burlap Hall – and one o~~f th~~e reasons the author so enjoyed writing this particular book was because she could turn "all the teachers from their pompous selves into ridiculous creatures." The book is something of a family affair, as the black and white illustrations are by Virginia's father, Christopher Ironside.

Virginia Ironside wrote her first novel – *Chelsea Bird* – when she was only eighteen. Since then she has worked as pop correspondent for the *Daily Mail*, problem page editor for *Woman* magazine and currently as agony aunt for the *Sunday Mirror*.

Virginia Ironside lives in west London with her teenage son.

Books for adults by Virginia Ironside

Chelsea Bird
Distant Sunset
Made for Each Other

How to Have a Baby and Stay Sane

VAMPIRE MASTER

"*I prefer to stand, if I may, dear sir,*" replied Mr
Culard, *drawing himself up in front of Mr Fox's desk.*

VAMPIRE MASTER

VIRGINIA IRONSIDE

Illustrated by
CHRISTOPHER IRONSIDE

WALKER BOOKS
LONDON

For William

First published 1987 by Walker Books Ltd
87 Vauxhall Walk, London SE11 5HJ

Text © 1987 Virginia Ironside
Illustrations © 1987 Christopher Ironside
Cover illustration by Mick Brownfield

This edition published 1989

Printed in Great Britain by Cox and Wyman Ltd, Reading
Typeset by Graphicraft Typesetters Ltd, Hong Kong

British Library Cataloguing in Publication Data
Ironside, Virginia
Vampire master.
I. Title   II. Ironside, Christopher
823'.914[F]
ISBN 0-7445-0840-1

CHAPTER ONE

"Look, I just don't want to take this Bible to school, Mum." Tom Buxton sighed as he saw a look of pleading coming over his mother's face. "It's too heavy and the school is knee-deep in Bibles as it is... Oh, *all right*!" he finished heatedly, grabbing it from her and hurling it into his suitcase. "All right, all right, if it'll make you happy!"

He'd been boarding at Burlap Hall for only four weeks at the end of the last summer term, thrown in among a whole crowd of kids he'd never met before, and the thought of going back made him miserable. The other kids were OK – at least it was a coeducational school with girls as well as boys – but it was being away from home for so long that filled him with gloom. He'd never wanted to go away to boarding school in the first place; he'd been perfectly happy at Grafton Park, the comprehensive down the road. His mother, he knew, wasn't happy about him boarding away, either; and his father would have preferred him at home. So why go?

It was all the fault of his father's sister, a miserable spinster with a nose like a carrot, whose one goal, apart from knitting big, woolly sweaters for the poor in Africa (What did they want with big woolly sweaters, anyway? Weren't they hot enough already?) had been to see that Tom was given what she called "a good chance in life". She'd died six months ago and in her will she'd made provision for Tom to attend Burlap Hall, a private boarding school where her own father had once been a pupil and where Tom, she felt, would be sure to do well in his GCSEs, and perhaps take A levels and then, maybe, gasp gasp, bring out the flags... GET INTO UNIVERSITY!

Tom's vision of university was that it all took place in rotting stone rooms in some decrepit old town with one cinema, and was peopled by a mixture of pompous young men who said "Yah" and listened to classical music, ridiculous old farts in black gowns who looked like crows and made jokes in Latin and ghastly, chubby girls whose idea of a good night out was drinking coffee while listening to long-haired actors reading Ted Hughes. As Tom had already decided that he was going to be the world's next Mr Amstrad and leave home early to earn more money than his father by selling television aerials off the back of his bicycle or some other money-making wheeze, he wanted to avoid university at all costs. But his parents had other ideas, brainwashed into believing that qualifications got you jobs – when everyone with anything up top knew that getting qualifications just wasted time that could be better spent making a fortune.

"Jobs are thin on the ground these days," declared his father, who'd spent his life clambering up a career ladder in the insurance business – a remarkably long ladder considering he was still earning only peanuts as a senior administrator. "I know you don't want to go away to school, but this really is a chance, Tom, and you'd be mad not to take it."

"I'll miss you so much," said his mother. "But be sensible, Tom. You're thirteen now, it'll only be for a few years, you'll come home in the holidays and it could make all the difference to your future. And then you'll be able to look after us in our old age," she added with a blackmailing smile.

Despite his own feelings of misery at returning to school, Tom felt a twinge of guilt over the argument about the Bible. His grandmother was seriously ill and his mother was even more worried and anxious than usual. And whenever there was death in the air, she'd always grab at any religious feeling she could get her hands on, like a good-luck charm – even though in normal circumstances she only visited a church to admire the stained glass windows. Although Tom rarely saw his grandmother, who had spent most of her later years in a nursing home, he knew her illness upset his mum.

"I'm sorry," said Tom, giving his mother a hug. "It's just that I hate Burlap Hall. The uniform alone!" he added, as his eyes fell to the bed on which lay, neatly folded, a hideous pair of Acrilan grey trousers, a Bri-Nylon grey jersey, a polyester grey shirt and a horrible pair of clumping, black shoes that made him look like a prison warder.

At least this was the Christmas term. Last term all the pupils had been compelled to wear shorts, and to spare himself the embarrassment of being seen by anyone in the local village, he'd confined himself to the school grounds for the weeks he was there.

"I do understand, pet," said his mother sympathetically. "But it's only eight weeks and you'll soon be home for Christmas." And with that she returned his hug and hurried out of his room, trying not to show how upset she felt herself.

Only eight weeks? Eight weeks seemed to Tom an exceptionally long time. It had been explained to him once that when you're one year old, a month seems ages because it's a twelfth of your whole life. When you're forty, a month is only one four hundred and eightieth of your whole life and as a result it flashes past. At thirteen, two months was one seventy-eighth of Tom's life and seemed a very long time indeed.

He looked at himself in the mirror. His hair was nicely spiked, covered with the special styling gel he'd bought with his birthday money; he sported a baggy short-sleeved shirt, covered with sunshades and pineapples (one that Errol, a friend from Grafton Park, had given him from the West Indies. No one at Burlap Hall knew anybody from the West Indies). His smart, grey, baggy trousers, caught in with fashionable elastic at the ankles, topped a cool pair of trainers – of the style strictly not allowed at Burlap Hall. At Burlap Hall you still had to wear things called "gym shoes" or "plimsolls", horrible, flat affairs with laces instead of Velcro.

He wouldn't be able to get into these clothes again for two months – or rather, for one seventy-eighth of his life – except, perhaps, at half-term when he'd be allowed home for a blissful few days. Tears came into Tom's eyes but he blinked them away. Then there'd be another seventy-eighth till Christmas. Then a few more seventy-eighths and by next year all the calculations would change because he'd be a year older and a term would be only one eighty-fourth of his life. Perhaps time would move a bit quicker then.

And there were some advantages to Burlap Hall, he had to admit. The terms were a lot shorter than at Grafton Park; he had become friendly with Miles Parker whose father was an immensely wealthy Harley Street doctor which meant that in the holidays Tom had had a couple of trips with him to West End films, followed by the sort of meals at pizza houses that Tom would normally only get to eat on his birthday. Miles' father would sometimes leave the odd tenner with his son to go out and hire a couple of films to see on one of their many video recorders – and the family had even offered to pay for Tom to go on a skiing trip with them the following Easter. At Grafton Park there wasn't a lot of entertaining and the best invitation was usually to go to someone's flat to "muck around" rather than be treated to an outing.

Then there was his other friend at Burlap Hall, Susan – although she was more Miles' friend than Tom's. She was an American, whose parents were diplomats in Rome. She was a lot more adult than most of the giggling girls at Burlap Hall and had a good line in feminist fury, always quick to point out any form of sexism. If she had a fault it was that she was not over-endowed with a sense of humour – but as Miles often pointed out she was endowed with other things, particularly in her chest area, which he insisted made up for it. Tom imagined that she must have been a thorn in the side of the teachers, but apparently her parents were extremely influential; and keeping her there was in the school's interest, since when her father was mentioned in the press, Burlap Hall got the odd plug in the process – always resulting in a pile of applications. No, there was no question, there was room for improvement at Burlap Hall – a huge fire, for one – but it wasn't as bad as all that.

Meanwhile, at Burlap Hall itself, Mr Fox, the headmaster, was going through his own traumas. He sat at his desk reading a letter. The autumn sun glimmered through the Gothic window behind him in which glowed in red stained glass the words:

NOLITE IGNARI ESSE

It meant "Do not be ignorant", but most pupils at Burlap Hall translated it to mean "Don't be a wally."

The sun shone on his domed head, over which a few sad locks of hair were carefully arranged to look as if he weren't bald on top, which, of course, he was. Like Tom, he was wearing his casual clothes, but they weren't quite as stylish. Casual clothes to Mr Fox meant a sagging, brown cardigan with leather buttons – or perhaps "button" would be a better way of describing it as there was only one, there being no Mrs Fox to sew them on since she'd run off with the local doctor five years ago. Underneath was a tight shirt that he must have bought in his thinner days, because he bulged out of it like a balloon in a body-stocking. He wore loud, flared, yellow trousers that were slightly too short and a pair of socks in ancient leather sandals. Tom would have thought that Mr Fox looked ridiculous (but there again, had Mr Fox seen Tom in his holiday clothes, he would have scoffed at

Tom as well). And in his own way Mr Fox was comfortable in his casual clothes and he, too, dreaded the next day when he would be obliged to don his worn suit and black gown. Sometimes he sneakily wore his comfortable cardigan and shirt underneath but he had to be careful no one spotted them.

On an old oak chest nearby was balanced a large cage, with a label attached to it, in which a couple of sad hamsters poked their noses from a dusty ball of bedding. Next to it was a tank of greenish-grey water in which floated a geriatric toad on a decaying raft of plastic; and perched on top of both of these was another cage in which five mice were crammed onto a wheel scurrying along as if they had a train to catch. With a deep sigh, Mr Fox perused the letter again.

Dear Mr Fox,
    I regret to inform you that I shall not be returning to Burlap Hall as biology teacher this term. I apologize for giving you such short notice but I joined a religious sect called the Church of Scientology yesterday and I am committing my life to the pursuit of the ends outlined by the great L. Ron Hubbard.
    Yours in harmony and peace,

Marisda Flumen R
(Cyril Cholmondely as was)

PS. We will meet in another life.
PPS. I am sending the laboratory animals under separate cover by special messenger. The hamsters need a handful of sunflower seeds each day; the toad needs one ounce of fresh meat and dead flies and the mice need grain, seeds and vegetables. Their cages and the tank should be cleaned weekly.

Mr Fox put his head in his hands with a groan. "Oh, pessimissimus," he whispered to himself. Why, oh, why did this have to happen to him? What had he done to deserve it? Was it retribution for the fact that when he had played croquet on the cricket pitch with a couple of friends in the holidays and the groundsman had complained of the holes, he'd blamed local boys for vandalism? Because he'd underpaid the blind piano tuner who'd visited the day before? Or was it because he'd altered the marks on Asquith Minor's exam papers to persuade his millionaire parents he was doing well enough to merit his staying on at Burlap Hall? (It was only sense: they'd promised to contribute to the new science block.) But whatever he'd done surely could not merit such punishment as this. These wretched animals! He peered over his desk at the toad which gave him a frightful froggy stare. He'd never trusted Cholmondely since he'd caught him going to church three times on Sundays, haring round the local parishes on his bike following the services at different churches in the neighbourhood. Once on Sundays – OK; three times on Sundays – definitely weird.

Well, there was nothing he could do about these animals. He didn't have dead flies, raw meat or sunflower seeds available to feed them with. (While he was right about the raw meat and sunflower seeds, there was actually a wide variety of dead flies to be found not only in a dusty corner of the cricket pavilion but lying roasting on the windowsill behind him.) He got up, went over to the bookcase, pulled out a copy of the Yellow Pages, discreetly hidden behind a row of a 1935 edition of the *Encyclopaedia Britannica* (it had nothing at all under H for Hitler) and looked up Biologists – between Bingo Eqpt and Biscuit Mfrs.

After several telephone calls he had no luck with a new biology teacher but he did find a laboratory where he intended taking the wretched animals.

The sun was shining after lunch as Mr Fox drove cautiously down the bumpy drive of Burlap Hall, a once delightful avenue of trees which had grown huge and out of shape due to lack of school funds to maintain them. The sight of a torn netball basket beyond reminded him of the irritating presence of girls at Burlap Hall – a money-making scheme introduced by his predecessor. Through the trees, the fields could be glimpsed like brown patchwork, occasionally textured by great rolls of straw, curled like giant Shredded Wheats; little clouds scudded to and fro and in the sky a kestrel shuddered as if waiting to swoop on its prey. Struck with the bizarre notion that perhaps it could smell the mice through the roof of his car, he revved the engine to pick up more speed, but a splashing sound from the back made him pull his foot off the accelerator.

He turned carefully into the road that led to the village, past the church, the village shop, the Olde Tea Shoppe, which sold all too olde sandwiches made of curling sliced bread filled with tinned ham and sliced processed cheese, past the vet, the one-pump petrol station, the doctor's surgery (where he always dangerously closed his eyes lest he should see his ex-wife laughing over the gate) and along till he hit the main road to Lanchester.

Lanchester Labs Ltd. was a dreary one-storey complex on the outskirts of the town; it was covered with corrugated iron and smelt of rat droppings – pessimissimus indeed. He parked outside a door marked DEPOT and after pressing a bell at the grimy office, he took the animals out of the car and waited. A gloomy-looking man appeared and pulled back a sliding glass window.

"Are you the man with the ruddy animals?" he growled, in a strong Lanchesterian accent. "Let's have a look-see then."

He sauntered outside to the forecourt, scoffingly glanced at the cages and sucked wheezingly on a slimy cigarette end that dangled from his mouth. "No ruddy use to anyone," he said. "Best throw them away down the lavvy. At least you can use the cages." He gave a gritty laugh that turned into a cough and then spat on the forecourt, missing Mr Fox's sandals by inches.

"Perhaps *you* could throw them away," suggested Mr Fox, who was squeamish about things like that. "You can keep the cages," he added.

"Yeah, nice cages," said the man, fingering them. "Where d'you get them? Off the back of a lorry? Want me to get rid of the evidence?" he added, with a cunning wink.

"Certainly not," replied Mr Fox, drawing himself up in his most dignified, headmasterly way and delivering one of his famous Fox looks. His eyes bulged with indignant fury, the hairs on his brow seemed to aim forwards like a row of tiny ray-guns, his ears moved outwards like sails on the Armada and his whole face seemed to grow bigger and redder, apparently about to explode. The man straightened up immediately as if he were worried that Mr Fox might give him double Latin prep as a punishment.

"I do beg your pardon, sir," he said, in a much modulated voice, producing an obsequious smile and straightening his stained tie. He slicked his cigarette around so that it was hidden in the palm of his hand. "I do apologize. On second thoughts, I'm sure I can find a place for these animals. There are several old people I know who would be glad of some companionship, the poor, sad, old dears. Lovely people. Or perhaps our local pre-school playgroup would be interested. You obviously are from a school, sir, now I see you closer."

"I am," said Mr Fox, pompously. "And I am in somewhat of a predicament," he added, suddenly struck by a brilliant thought. "You don't happen to know of any spare biology teachers, do you?" He mentioned it as if at laboratories you could order biology teachers by the hundredweight. "My own biology teacher has given in his resignation today, the day before term starts, and I'm in a ruddy fix."

This sudden lapse into rather more pally language made the man nervous – in the way that boys feel when talked to as an equal by their headmaster. It always smells of a trap.

"Since you mention it, sir," said the man, with another ghastly smile, "I've just this minute supplied someone with animals who was looking for a biology post. Just arrived from abroad, sir, the middle of Europe somewhere. He asked me to look out for something for him and left me his card. I've got it here somewhere. Funny chap," he said, rummaging in his pockets. "Very pale face and red mouth, almost as if he'd got make-up on. But extremely polite, a real gentleman. Ah, yes," he said, revealing a grimy piece of card printed in red. "Here it is." Mr Fox snatched it from his hand. A godsend! It read:

Mr. A. Culard
Expert in Biology and Related Subjects
666, Gravesend Road
Lanchester

He gave hurried thanks, leapt into his car and drove off at great speed.

The man on the forecourt was left scratching his head in puzzlement. That was funny, he thought. How could Mr Culard live at 666 Gravesend Road? His own sister lived in Gravesend Road and he could swear there weren't more than thirty houses in it, because hers was number thirty, the very last in the row. It was all very queer. But then Mr Culard himself had been very queer, come to that. What on earth was he planning to do with the cages of animals he'd bought from Lanchester Labs earlier – five hundred rats and three caseloads of bats?

CHAPTER TWO

Burlap Hall was a frenzy of activity on the first day of term. Range Rovers drew up in the drive, dwarfing the Jaguars and Bentleys that were already parked. The air was filled with the sounds of people talking and yelling, mingled with the excited yaps of family dogs. A huge coach stood with its engine still shuddering as boys and girls who'd been collected from the station piled out and greeted other friends. A frantic driver was hauling the luggage – suitcases, tuckboxes, tennis rackets, cellos, fencing foils, hockey-sticks – from the boot, and Mr Fritz, the science master, stood in the drive with a clipboard, ticking off names and chatting to parents, trying to take notes and sort out their problems at the same time.

"...allergic to wheat, so it's very important that she sticks to a special diet...", "...mustn't swim without goggles, as his eyes...", "...leave two days before the end of term, as we're going on a world cruise...", "...husband and I were divorced in the holidays and I'm expecting him to pay the fees, so let me know if...", "...having another baby, so if she seems a bit anxious it's to be expected..."

The jabber of parental instructions floated through the stained glass window of Mr Fox's study where he was attempting to juggle the timetable for the eighth time that afternoon. He'd got it right the previous day but, as individual teachers arrived and made their own special demands, it had had constantly to be altered. "But I can't possibly teach five hours on the go without a break!" or "If you're expecting me to face 2C twice

21

in one day you've got another think coming. No way, no way, no way." Not to mention "But let's say it rains on Thursday afternoons, how can I give the kids gym if you've booked the hall for detention pupils at the same time?"

Each objection brought a new headache for Mr Fox. But at least he'd got the biology teacher sorted out. Though the whole business had been most peculiar.

He'd arrived at Gravesend Road to find there was no number 666 and had returned to the school in despair, muttering "pessimissimus" all the way back. He'd made a series of abortive phone calls to various neighbouring schools and agencies, but was interrupted by the arrival of Signor Ruzzi, the music teacher, who had taken the early train in order to be able to check that the piano was in tune. (Last term he'd made a frightful fuss when he found the B flat was flat and had threatened to resign on the spot. Mr Fox couldn't understand it. He thought B flat was *meant* to be flat.)

When Mr Fox had reassured him that it had been tuned the previous day and had listened to a recital of the latest piano pieces that Signor Ruzzi had decided to include in this term's curriculum (not to mention a recital of all Signor Ruzzi's problems in getting to Burlap Hall and how the guard on the train had made him pay an extra fare because his cello took up an entire seat), he hurried back to his office to continue the search for a biology teacher – and was taken aback to find his window slightly open.

To make matters even more mysterious, a yellowing envelope lay on his desk with his name written on it in red ink.

Inside was a letter penned in a scrawly handwriting, which read:

22

My dear Mr Fox,

A thousand apologies for the difficulties I have caused you with regard to my present abode. A little ~~bat~~ bird has told me that you are in need of a biology teacher this term. May I offer my humble services? I have a triple degree in biology from the University of Bistrita which I received with honours in 1645. I am eager to teach your pupils and hope very much that they will be able to drink from the fountain of my knowledge. If I may I will visit you in the late afternoon on the first day of term and hope very much that you will require my services.

Assuring you of my good wishes at all times, I remain,

A. Culard

PS. I will bring my own laboratory animals with me as I gather you have disposed of yours.

Presumably, thought Mr Fox, he must have meant 1945. He hoped Mr Culard wasn't dyslexic. He could see he'd had trouble with the word "bird" in the letter. First he'd written "bat" but had crossed it out. And Heaven knows how the man had ever managed to get the letter to him because he could have sworn it hadn't been there when he left his desk. But no matter. All that concerned him was the fact that a biology teacher was coming after all.

After a distressing parting from his parents on the station platform and last minute instructions to them on how to look after his hamster, Tom arrived at

Burlap station and took the coach with the others. He chatted to Rosemary about her ballet lessons, heard about Simon's new computer and had to listen to Sheila describing a new litter of puppies her dog had given birth to on her bed. But the person he really wanted to see was Miles and he was disappointed not to see his freckled face among the twittering throng in the school driveway — until he heard a call from an upstairs window.

"Hiya, Tom!" was the call — though it sounded more like "Hiyah" — and Tom knew it must be Miles. He looked up and saw him waving from a Gothic window surrounded by ivy. The autumn sun glinted on the braces on his teeth. "Over here! You're sharing a room with me this term! It's absolutely brill! Come up and have a look!"

Great, thought Tom as he hurried into the huge, cold hall and raced up the stairs, almost slipping on the new polish. He looked around on the landing upstairs, confused, when a battered, oak door burst open and Miles popped his head out, grinning at him.

"In here, old chap," he said and welcomed Tom into a snug little room with two beds, two desks and a wash-basin. "And look what I've smuggled in," said Miles, whipping a tiny object that looked like a calculator from behind his back. It was a Sinclair mini-television, strictly not allowed at Burlap Hall. "Now we'll be able to watch all the late programmes," he said. "And even *Night Thoughts* if we want, which we won't. I came down early and bagged this room before anyone else could get it. Because, you know, there are only three of these. Hope you like it," he added anxiously.

"It's excellent," said Tom, heaving his suitcase onto

the bed nearest the window. He was really pleased. This room couldn't be better. One thing he'd particularly loathed about the term before was sleeping in a long dormitory with rows of other boys, most of whom had smelly feet. There was no privacy, and if you wanted just to sit and have a private think, there was always the risk of Asquith Minor throwing a wet sponge at you in mid-mull.

"Last term I felt I couldn't even dream in private. But here...well," he said generously, "I don't mind *you* looking in on my dreams, Miles."

"Heh, heh, depends what they're about, eh?" leered Miles, making a squeezing motion with his hands. He opened his suitcase and revealed a pile of cuttings of Page Three girls from the *Sun*. "Let's cover the walls with them," he suggested. "Or would you prefer them in colour?" He fished out some copies of *Playboy* from underneath a pair of striped pyjamas.

Just as they were both engrossed in examining every photo, chortling over the girls' bottoms and boobs, there was a light knock on the door and Susan peeked in, her crimped red hair bursting from her head.

"Hi, guys," she said, closing the door behind her. "Have good holidays? I'm in the room just over the corridor sharing with Rosemary and about five hundred pairs of ballet shoes. It's a real drag to be back, isn't it?" Tom thought it was more of a drag that she had just come in, but was amused to see Miles immediately sitting on his *Playboy*s and pushing the *Sun* cuttings out of view.

"Did you hear Mr Cholmondely's left?" said Miles, slipping easily into school conversation.

"No, but anyone could tell he wasn't right," said Susan, tossing her head and sitting down between them on the bed. "Church three times a day on Sunday? There was a freak and a half."

"At least we won't have to listen to him singing hymns in his bath any more," said Tom, who'd found it hard to sleep with strains of "To Be a Pilgrim" floating through the air every night.

"You mean hers, not hymns," said Susan, automatically. "We don't want any sexist talk round here. Hey, what on earth's this?" she added, looking down. A picture of an enormous, bulbous breast was sticking out under Miles' bottom. She tugged at it violently, making Miles nearly topple over. When she saw what it was she exploded. "You *dirty guys*!" she shrieked. "You're the most sexist people I know. Don't you realize you're treating women as sex objects?" She jumped up and looked at them pityingly. "You know what you're going to grow up into? Dirty old men! A menace to society!"

"Don't you mean a womanace to society?" asked Miles, jumping off the bed and taking melodramatic refuge behind the cupboard.

Susan leapt on Tom, pinning him to the wall. "I've got your friend!" she shouted. "I've got your friend! I'm torturing him to de—eath! Unless you apologi—ize. Listen, Miles, he's screaming for he—elp!"

Even though she'd interrupted them, Tom couldn't help laughing so much he hardly heard the bell. But its deafening sound was soon reverberating round the whole school.

"Time for our measly rations," said Miles, grinning as he appeared from behind the cupboard. Susan let go her hold of Tom and got up, shaking her fist at him. "I'll get you one day," she said, aimiably. "You wait till you find me gloating over pictures of sexy males, then you won't find it so funny!"

"Isn't she gorgeous?" said Miles to Tom, with an exaggerated sigh, as she left. "Almost worth coming back to school for. And did you notice how she'd grown?" he added meaningfully.

"Don't think I didn't hear that!" Susan's voice came floating down the corridor. "You just wait!"

Perhaps Burlap Hall wasn't quite as bad as Tom had made out. Even Susan, who insisted on tagging along with them all the time, had her good moments.

It was in the middle of tea, during Mr Fox's second buttered scone (he'd consumed his first surreptitiously on his own in his study because he didn't like to encourage greed among his pupils), that he began to get a bit nervous about the biology teacher. He looked at his watch under the table, hoping that Mrs Grain, the Latin teacher, who was sitting next to him, wouldn't notice.

"But I assure you," she was saying, "that although you may use the word 'pessimissimus' as a *humorous* expression of disgust, there is no such word in the Latin. The superlative of 'malus' is simply 'pessimus' – the comparative, of course, being 'peior' or, as we would say, 'worse'."

Mr Fox nodded, wondering when she would stop yapping. Where on earth *was* that Mr Culard? It was already getting dark outside and the huge neon strips, dangling from the ancient Gothic ceiling, were starting to flicker into life, giving out a yellowish-greenish light that made all the pupils and staff look ill and strained. Even the jam looked a funny colour.

There was a distant chime and Mr Fox perked up. Perhaps that was him. He helped himself to another cup of tea and looked expectantly at the door. Relief! The secretary was signalling to him that he had a visitor, so he excused himself and, taking his tea with him, went upstairs to welcome his guest.

At first, all Mr Fox could discern was a tall, thin figure in a dark corner by the bookcases, its arms crossed over its chest. He could make out its long, black outline and a pale, silvery face staring into nothingness. When he snapped on the light the figure gave a horrified start, but recovered itself quickly.

"Mr Culard? I hope I have the pleasure?" said Mr Fox, bowing slightly in the figure's direction as he went round to his desk and sat down. "Do please take a seat," he added, gesturing to the chair in front of him.

"I prefer to stand, if I may, dear sir," replied Mr Culard, drawing himself up in front of Mr Fox's desk.

Now he could see him clearly, Mr Fox gave a slight start. For Mr Culard was a singularly repulsive-looking man. About six feet six inches tall, he had a face as grey as the ashes of a bonfire, with two dark coals for eyes, surrounded by dark, red, gleaming sockets. His mouth was a contrast, a bright, glittering slash of red that covered shiny, white pointed teeth. His hair was, or had been, red: long, lank locks of it fell limply past grey, pointed ears, and onto the collar of his greasy, black coat. His white, bony hands clutched at each other across his chest and his long, dirty fingernails pressed into the glassy skin of his wrists.

"By all means," replied Mr Fox, feeling at a great disadvantage as he gazed up into the man's face. He was used to towering above his guests, for whom he always provided particularly low chairs.

"Now, ah, biology," he said, sitting up extremely straight to give himself extra height. "As you have probably gathered, I have been let down by my old biology teacher – he was always a religious man but he suddenly joined the Church of Scientology on the spur of the moment, leaving me completely high and dry." He gave a hearty laugh to try to make this sound jocular, in order to lighten the atmosphere which seemed to have acquired a deadly, frozen feel.

"I am not a church-going man myself," said Mr Culard, giving a grim smile. "You need have no fears of anything similar happening in my case. No fears at all," he added, with a ghastly, wheezy laugh that sounded like the whistling of wind through a graveyard. But despite his appearance, his voice was pleasant enough even with its strong Middle-European accent, thought Mr Fox. Deep and rich as if it had been matured for centuries, like old whisky.

Mr Fox rose, to make himself feel more at ease, and settled his bulky figure on top of his desk. "Have you had much experience of teaching?" he asked. "Because obviously some of our pupils will be taking their GCSEs next year and we have a reputation to keep up. I trust you are aware of the current curriculum."

"I have years and years of experience," droned Mr Culard, in his reassuringly hypnotic voice, fixing Mr Fox with a penetrating stare. Mr Fox felt pinned to the spot by the look in his eyes and froze like a girl in a circus faced by a knife-thrower.

"I have coached students throughout the world for cemetries," continued Mr Culard, "I mean centuries. I mean, of course, that it *seems* like centuries! I have taught the sons of kings and the daughters of peasants. I have taught the high and the low, the rich and the poor. I have studied animal life for nights on end. I have had personal experience of dissection, examination and even digestion. I mean I have personal experience of the digestive systems of animals throughout the world. No pupil of mine has ever failed my examinations. Not only am I an expert in every field of biology but after a few lessons I can assure you that my pupils generally become my disciples, many begging for extra tuition at nights. And talking of nights, I have one problem. I suffer from a rare disease − not at all contagious you will be glad to hear − that affects my skin. You may have noticed my distinctive pallor. I suffer from Luminosis, an allergy to daylight. Although when I feel strong I can work reasonably well in the day, I am at my best in the hours of darkness, after about five o'clock at this time of year. And so I would request, if it is at all possible, that I deliver my lessons in the afternoon and evening, rather than in the morning. I hope this will be to your satisfaction."

Mr Fox groaned inwardly. These teachers! He would now have to reorganize the timetable all over again, just when he'd got all the copies finalized and photostatted. Still, beggars couldn't be choosers and he'd simply have to start again, even if it meant working through the night.

"To be honest, it isn't very convenient," he replied with a sigh. "But obviously I would not like to exacerbate your condition. I will do my best. Now, about your fees..."

"My dear sir, I teach only for the love of it," said Mr Culard. "And because I am putting you out by my unusual request in the matter of my working hours, let us keep the fees low. Say, twenty pounds a week? And have no fears about my accommodation, by the way. I have taken rooms in the village and will take my meals there. Just give me the times of my lessons and I assure you I will never let you down."

Mr Fox could hardly believe his ears. Twenty smack-eroos a week? And he'd save on food as well. And laundry. And he wouldn't have to listen to all his complaints at mealtimes. Or his gossip. Mr Culard might look a bit weird but all in all the headmaster felt he'd got himself a very good deal. He slipped down off the desk-top and shook Mr Culard by the hand. It was ice-cold and he could feel the teacher's fingernails like vultures' claws: hard, damp and chilly.

"Done!" he exclaimed. "And now, let me offer you a drink!" He went over to his bookcase and removed a couple of copies of Lowe's *Latin Primer* to reveal an array of bottles. "A glass of Liebfraumilch?" he suggested. "A sweet, German wine?"

Behind him Mr Culard's voice hummed, deep and misty. "My good sir, what a kind thought. And a wine from Middle-Europe, my homeland. I am charmed."

Mr Fox, offering him a glass, thought Mr Culard looked even taller than before.

"But I am afraid," added Mr Culard, waving his hand in a negative gesture, "I will be compelled to refuse."

A curious, dusty smell filled the room and Mr Fox felt slightly faint. "You see," Mr Culard continued, smiling mysteriously, his red lips stretching over his white teeth, "I never drink... wine."

CHAPTER THREE

The first assembly of term at Burlap Hall was the day when Mr Fox, resplendent in his newly dry-cleaned black gown, ascended the platform in the big hall and outlined to the school his master-plan for the term. The air was unhealthy, thought Tom, as he stood, squashed among hundreds of bodies, the backs of his calves pressing uncomfortably against the iron bar of his school chair. The hall smelt of pencils, sweat, old chewing-gum and cabbage already being boiled to a soggy mush in the school kitchens. Oh, Lord. Second lesson that morning was geography and he *still* hadn't finished the holiday homework Mr Roy had set at the end of last term. How *did* one extract coal from a mine? What *was* the composition of a river bed? And would he ever need to know it in later life? Unless he were caught in a hurricane in the fast sports car he planned to buy one day and wild winds blew it off a bridge he was crossing, Tom couldn't think that he'd ever get anywhere near a river bed. He was jolted from his daydream by the sound of his name, booming out over the hall. "And Tom Buxton, one of our newer friends at Burlap Hall, will be head monitor for class 2C. He has already impressed us with his friendliness and cooperation," droned Mr Fox. Through a desultory round of applause Miles whispered: "Hard luck, old cheese. You know it means you have to get up quarter of an hour earlier, don't you, to check the classroom?"

Tom groaned inside. Mr Fox had obviously made him head monitor to "give him a sense of belonging", the last thing he wanted.

Mr Fox's voice changed to a more sombre tone. "And I have great sadness in telling you that Mr Cholmondely will not be with us this term. He has left for personal reasons and we will all miss him greatly. But we are very lucky to be able to welcome Mr Culard who has travelled all the way from... from..." (Where the hell *did* he come from? wondered Mr Fox.) "From— ah— afar, to help us out with biology this term. He is widely experienced and assures me he has even taught the sons of princes in his time, so I am relying on you to give a good impression!" There was a dreary ripple of sycophantic laughter. Next to Tom, Susan muttered: "And what about the daughters of princes might I ask? I suppose they were all killed at birth."

More waffle concluded the talk which covered the state of the grass on the big lawn, the fact that everyone must keep their lockers secure because of an outbreak of thefts last term, a warning not to talk to strangers in the village, a new and mad rule that the colour of the laces of pupils' plimsolls had to conform to the colour of the actual shoe, and then the announcement of various events, like the school concert, the annual school photograph and the Harvest Festival.

"This year especially," concluded Mr Fox, "I have high hopes of the Harvest Festival exceeding all other years in terms of produce, happiness and, of course, warm-heartedness. As you know, all the produce donated will go to deserving old folk in the village who find it hard to keep body and soul together on their small pensions. It is up to each and every one of us to help them by the generosity we produce, both in what we give in terms of produce and also, in our heartfelt... ah, heartfeltedness." Mr Fox wondered if he hadn't rather gone over the top. He'd also used the word "produce" too often.

("Body and soul my foot," whispered Miles to Tom. "Last year I staggered down to the village with a great basket of cauliflowers and marrows and when I knocked on this old wrinklie's door, he put it on a chain, peered out, stared into my basket and said: 'What, more bloody marrows? Do us a favour, sonny, next time make it baked beans and a bottle of Scotch.' And he slammed the door on me.")

"I hope you heard me, Parker!" boomed Mr Fox, spotting Miles' lips move from the other side of the hall. "You'd better listen carefully because I won't be repeating this."

"Thank goodness," whispered Susan.

Eventually the harangue came to an end and Signor Ruzzi, who had been looking extemely bored throughout the whole performance and had been dreaming of conducting *La Traviata* to stupendous applause at the Rome Opera House, was nudged by Mrs Grain and promptly started playing the school song, the Burlap Anthem, to which he had written a new arrangement in the holidays, full of jerky dissonants, wild plink-plonk noises where no one expected them and a finale of a deliberately loud and discordant seventh. Mr Fox vowed to have a word with him about it, but then changed his mind when he remembered the last time he had dared criticize one of the Signor's *œuvres*. Finally it ended and with a great squeaking of chairs and a burst of chatter everyone left for their various classrooms.

Tom was relieved that Mr Fritz, the science teacher, took the first lesson — about the only member of staff who was human. He was an amiable old eccentric of around sixty who sported a goatee beard and half-moon spectacles. He rode a bicycle which he had designed and made himself, he smoked a pipe which he had designed and made himself and he wore a brown hairy suit which made him look like a hedgehog, which he had also designed and made himself. His shoes were a strange pair of leather moccasins which, yes, he had designed and made himself. After asking everyone about their holidays he told the class about his – he'd been on a trip to Romania. That was what Tom liked about him – he didn't go straight into the lesson, yelling at everyone. And when he was cross – which he seldom was – his worst punishment was to tell the person who had misbehaved to repeat after him: "I am a stupid boy." Or girl, as Susan would say.

"And now, I'm afraid I shall have to teach you something," he said, after he'd collected the holiday snapshots that he'd proudly handed round, "because you've got to pass your exams. And if you don't pass your exams, I'll get the old heave-ho. And as I don't want to get the old heave-ho, I've got to get you through." This seemed to be perfectly reasonable to Tom. He was quite happy to learn science to stop Mr Fritz getting the old heave-ho.

"Today, metamorphosis," said Mr Fritz, wearily dragging a large folder in front of him. "Metamorphosis is the action or process of changing in form. An example of this is the tadpole which changes into a frog. Can any of you think of any other examples?"

There was a general flinging up of arms.

"A caterpillar turning into a butterfly?" asked Asquith Minor.

"Very good."

"Water turning into ice?"

"No, metamorphosis is a permanent change."

"Wood turning into coal?" asked Simon.

"No, that is more a case of decay than metamorphosis." There was a silence. "There are many more of course," said Mr Fritz. "But then it's easy for me because I have in front of me a huge list of examples and you haven't."

"Glue turning into a hard lump?" The boy next to Simon had been bursting to speak.

"No," said Mr Fritz.

"Milk turning to yogurt?" said Sheila.

"No."

"A car turning into a lane?" suggested Miles.

Mr Fritz frowned. "Parker!" he said. "Say after me..."

"After me," said Miles.

Mr Fritz smiled faintly and continued: "I am a very stupid boy."

"Oh, I wouldn't say that, sir," said Miles, cheekily. "I think you're rather bright."

Mr Fritz smiled. "Thank you, Miles. I'm grateful for any compliments I can lay my hands on. However, we must get some more examples of metamorphosis. Any other ideas?"

Tom racked his brains. He hadn't contributed anything. Then his hand shot up. "What about vampires turning into bats?" he said.

There was general laughter, particularly from

Rosemary and a number of her friends but Mr Fritz looked serious.

"Vampires are no laughing matter," he said, sombrely. "In the Romanian village I was visiting these past holidays, for example, many of the villagers still believe in vampires and garland their windows with garlic to protect themselves."

"Ugh, yuk, pongy pongy," said Asquith Minor, clamping his nostrils together. "I hate garlic."

"So do vampires," said Mr Fritz, eyeing him sharply. "They also hate running water, sunlight, twigs of whitethorn, wild rose and the sign of the cross. And there's fire. They don't like that."

"Do you believe in them, sir?" asked Tom.

"Whether I believe in them or not is beside the point. Many people *do* believe in them. And to get back to your point about metamorphosis, of course the word is not only used in scientific terms. Metamorphosis takes place in a lot of myths and fairy stories. Witness Lot's wife who was turned to a pillar of salt – metamorphosis. Or Tantalus' daughter who was turned into a tree by the Gods. Same again. And of course in fairy stories princes are always being turned into toads by their wicked stepmothers and so on."

("Why aren't *princesses* ever turned into toads?" moaned Susan. "Sexist. Not fair." "There'd be no point in your case," whispered Miles, kindly. "You look like a toad already." Susan glowered.)

"However," said Mr Fritz, "this isn't getting us anywhere. Back to work. More examples, please."

But at that moment the bell rang.

"Oh, how will I ever teach you anything?" sighed Mr Fritz. "You'll never pass your exams. Heave-ho, here I come." He sadly gathered up his books and moved on to his next class.

The science lesson was followed by geography with Mr Roy, a health fanatic who insisted on the window being wide open for lessons. He himself seemed oblivious of the cold, perhaps because he wore thermal vests. One boy had once reported seeing flashes of light from his room at night and although it was rumoured that the healthy Mr Roy was actually a secret cigarette addict, the truth emerged that the flashes of light were the crackling of static as he removed his many layers of protective clothing. Throughout lessons he picked at a heap of sunflower seeds – he was a strict vegetarian – which he kept on his desk in an old yogurt pot; and occasionally, when the class was absorbed in supervised work, he would rise from his desk and fling his arms backwards and forwards – to keep his muscles elastic, he said.

Today it was trade in Europe. "And as I was horrified, last term, to discover that some of you don't yet know where all the countries in Europe actually are, I'd like you to start by copying the map of Europe on the wall into your notebooks," he said in his high, thin voice. "By next lesson I want you to know the names and the outlines of each and every country…"

Tom sighed, got out his pencil and laboriously started copying the countries from the large map which was flapping in the breeze. How he hated school! What on earth was the point of learning the shapes of the countries of the world when you could always look them up on a map? After all, if he were to find himself in, say, Spain and wanted to drive to Germany, he would hardly rely on his memory to get him there. He would buy a map and follow the roads. And the countries in the world kept changing their names anyway, so why bother to learn them? His mother had occasionally mentioned Persia and the Gold Coast which apparently didn't even exist now; and his dad still talked of going on holiday to Cumberland and Westmorland and even in Tom's short lifetime they'd vanished from the map. No doubt London itself would be called Meadvale or something when he was grown up. As he wearily drew the outlines of the countries and filled in the names, Tom decided it would be very bad for his future to let any of the information sink in.

Break followed and as Miles had been sent to the village to pick up a package for Mr Fox (probably his cigarettes, Tom thought), Susan came over to talk to him. He never quite understood what Miles saw in Susan. The way she droned on about feminism rather bored him – but Miles, he knew, fancied her. From the way Susan behaved, even though she was always putting him down, it occurred to Tom that she possibly fancied Miles back. Although he could hardly blame her for wanting to tag along with them all the time. He and Miles *were* after all the most brilliant, amusing, delightful and original people in the whole school. And had Tom been a girl he was sure he wouldn't have wanted to natter about pop stars and make-up all day like Rosemary and Sheila.

"Never share a room with a ballerina," said Susan languidly, as she leaned against the radiator by the wall beside him.

"I wasn't planning to," said Tom. "I don't even know any."

"I mean Rosemary, the would-be Margot Pavlova or whatever her name is," said Susan. "Do you know what a *pas de deux* is?"

"No couples allowed?"

Susan laughed. "No, it's some silly ballet step where you put your feet like this, I think," she said, showing him. "But why bother? If you want to get from A to B it's far easier to walk ordinarily." But Rosemary had shimmered over to them, drawn by the sight of Susan pointing her toes.

"I was showing him a *pas de deux*," said Susan, rather rudely.

"*That*'s not a *pas de deux*," said Rosemary, disparagingly. "A *pas de deux*," – and to make things worse she pronounced it with an immaculate French accent – "means the steps, *pas*, of two people, *deux*. A little ballet duet."

"Let's see you do an arabesque," said Susan, winking at Tom when Rosemary wasn't looking. Rosemary twirled around delighted to show off.

"Doesn't look very Arab to me," said Tom. And Rosemary flounced off in a sulk.

"Can you imagine putting up with that day after day?" sighed Susan. "Sometimes I've thought of putting thistles in her ballet shoes."

"At least you'd improve her jumps that way," said Tom and was flattered when Susan laughed loudly.

Actually Susan was OK when Miles wasn't around. But two was company and three was a crowd. At least she wasn't sharing their room.

"I wish I was sharing a room with you and Miles, instead of Rosemary," said Susan, as if reading his thoughts. "That'd be cool."

Tom thought it would be hot rather than cool, but he said nothing, just muttered "Mmm" vaguely and turned away. But their conversation was interrupted anyway by Mr Carstairs coming over to suggest a run. He was the English teacher who also took games.

"As long as it's a run and not a dance, I'll do it," said Susan and went off to change her shoes.

Mr Carstairs had rosy, red cheeks, a muscular body, ate heartily (or rather, noshed, as he would call it) and was tremendously enthusiastic about everything. As the whole class set off at a brisk jog down the big lawn, round the long meadow beyond, through the copse, over the brook and back up the long avenue, he started up a conversation with Tom.

"Absolutely *super* news about you being head monitor," he enthused. "Really well done! Congratulations!"

Tom smiled politely as he jogged, trying to dream up something to say. Mr Carstairs was already getting up speed and they were now hurtling into the long meadow beyond the lawn.

It was funny about talking to teachers. With Miles he could chatter on for hours, but the minute a teacher started up a conversation with him his mind froze into a paralysed lump. How did adults start conversations anyway? He could hardly say to Mr Carstairs: "My, my, how you have grown!" Nor would "And are you enjoying school?" seem really appropriate. And "What do you want to be when you grow up?" wouldn't do at all. Eventually, after desperately scratching around in his brain like a chicken looking for corn, he thought of something.

"Have you met Mr Culard, sir?" he asked. "What's he like?'

"No, none of us have," shouted Mr Carstairs as he ran. "He's a bit of a mystery character, in fact. He's apparently got some allergy to sunlight called Luminosis which means he can only teach in the afternoons and he's not staying in the school, he's taking rooms in

41

the village. Pity, that, because I think it's important that the teachers live and breathe the school and get really *involved* in all the activities."

There was silence as they continued running down by the hedge. The rest of Tom's class had fallen behind.

"By the way, we've got this absolutely *super* Shakespeare play to do this term," yelled Mr Carstairs to Tom as they entered the copse, puffing. Actually, only Tom puffed; Mr Carstairs took everything in his stride. "Ever read *Othello*? You'll love it. It's not so much a Shakespeare play as a thriller. It's really *exciting*. There's a wonderful bad man in it, just the sort of person Lee Marvin would play in a film." (Presumably some ancient sixties star, thought Tom, as he tried in vain to imitate Mr Carstairs' nifty leap over the stream and ended up clambering foolishly over the stones.) "And this *tremendously* hip black guy called Othello, reminds me rather of Sam Cooke, absolutely *doomed*, not to mention this *incredibly* sexy lady called Desdemona, you know she's a real star, like Marrona, you know who I mean?"

"Madonna, sir," gasped Tom. Trust Mr Carstairs to get it wrong.

They burst out of the copse through a bramble hedge and started up the avenue. Miles and his other friends were nowhere to be seen but he could hardly lag behind to wait for them in the middle of a conversation with Mr Carstairs.

"Madonna, that's right. I think the whole class will love it, it's so exciting, you really should just read it for pleasure, you won't be able to put it down." But Tom resolved not to be fooled this term. Last term Mr Carstairs had really raved about Jane Austen, giving her such a build-up that Tom actually bought a copy of

Pride and Prejudice with his own pocket money. And what had he got? A pathetic book about love that was *so boring* that he thought his brain might shrivel up into a tiny ball and roll out of his ear like a pea.

At last they were back at the school drive, the rest of the class far behind. Mr Carstairs looked puzzled. "Where are the others?" he asked, scratching his head. "Crumbs! Miles away! How about doing the run again and catching them up from behind? Come on, let's go!" And he was off like a greyhound, leaving Tom collapsed on the drive, taking off his shoes and letting the cool gravel trickle through his toes.

It was much later, after tea, that the class had their first encounter with Mr Culard. Outside it was just beginning to darken slightly and the lights and shades were starting to merge into one, so you could hardly distinguish between the trees and the sky. The glass on the window was cold and grey and the pupils shifted their desks to the middle of the room for warmth.

Finally there were footsteps outside and the door opened very slowly, with a creaking sound. Everyone stared expectantly. And in came the gaunt figure of Mr Culard, holding a huge cage in his hands.

There was a slight gasp of horror from the class when they saw him. He had a huge, pale bony nose, with greasy, red hairs sticking from black nostrils; his hands looked as big as plates and were covered with a dirty film, as if he'd been washing up in old grease. His teeth were sharp and white and from his mouth came a rank smell of bad breath as he stared at them. All in all he looked like a huge scarecrow, the bones in his body making awkward peaks in his black, greasy clothes.

He put the cage on the desk and sat down behind it,

peering through the bars at the class.

"Good evening, my young friends," he intoned, in his dark, velvety voice. "I cannot express how delighted I am to have the honour of introducing you to the wonderful, fascinating and mysterious world of biology. No!" he snapped sharply at Tom, who as class monitor had politely gone over to the door to turn on the light now it was too dark to see clearly. "No light! Please! My specimens will be disturbed. I appreciate your kindness, my young friend," he added, turning a ghastly smile on Tom as he skulked back to his desk, "but just today, or the next few days, until I feel a little stronger, I would prefer the light to be off.

"Now, you are all probably saying to yourselves: 'And what has kind Mr Culard brought us to examine this term? What is our special subject in biology going to be? Will it be hamsters?' So boring, I find! Though, of course, delicious. 'Or will it be frogs?' Too green and slimy, I think, do you not agree? But then, you will ask, 'What strange animals is kind Mr Culard planning to discuss?' Well, I will enlighten you, my young friends – if enlighten is the word to use in the secret world of darkness preferred by my animal friends in here," he added.

"I am sure that many of you are wondering what these bats like to eat. I will tell you. They eat insects, like flies and moths. Insects which are *alive*! I have caught some myself in a special trap and you may be interested to see them feeding. Gather round."

Some of the class got up to look, Simon and Asquith Minor struggling to be at the front, but others hung back. Tom dithered. He stood up and watched over the heads of the others and saw Mr Culard dip his bony hand into a brown paper bag and then put his clenched fist inside the cage. He slowly uncurled his fingers and out flew a dozen or so flies buzzing pathetically. The bats swooped on them and Tom could swear he heard a tiny munching sound as they gobbled their prey. The buzzing of the flies ceased and Tom felt sick.

"Oh, the poor flies!" some of the girls whimpered. "Oh, it's cruel!"

"Oh, I don't like it! It's 'orrible!" Sheila burst into noisy tears.

Mr Culard looked up menacingly. "It is not horrible," he intoned. "Life must feed on life. Or there will be no life. Eating the insects when they are alive gives my bats strength. Special strength. Let me show you." And he picked up the paper bag, threw his head back and, banging on the end of the bag, threw the remaining flies into his mouth. He slurped and chomped and licked his lips as gasps of horror and surprise rose from the whole class. The less sensitive members were somewhat impressed.

Tom was most upset. This was a completely different biology class to the ones Cholmondely used to give. He just wrote on the board and pointed to parts of his animals' bodies with a piece of chalk to show how they worked. But a biology teacher who ate live flies! There was something deeply creepy about such a display.

"Of course they find insects by themselves when they are hunting," continued Mr Culard, wiping a fly's wing from his lip as if nothing had happened. "And all the time they produce a shrill, continuous squeak which can be heard by man." He rattled the cage and there was a slight rustle and squeaking from within. "It is time, I think, for these bats to wake up and go out to feast on the insects of the night. Open the window, please," he snapped at Tom. "And we will see them leave." Tom went to the window and opened it. As he did so, the sound of the Lower Fourth's choir practice wafted up into the classroom.

Holy, holy, holy, merciful and mighty,
God in three persons, blessed Trinity.

Their high-pitched voices sounded so sweet in the night air that Tom stopped a moment to listen to them. But he was jerked from his concentration by an angry snarl from Mr Culard. He turned round and there was the teacher, who had shot up from his seat, his red eyes flashing and his face suffused with white rage.

"What's that evil noise?" he growled, in a low, threatening voice. "How can my bats go out when their night air is bombarded with this sound! It is polluting the air! It is preposterous!" His outburst was accompanied by a frightful squeaking from inside the cage and Tom could see that the bats were all fluttering about, huddling against a far corner.

"It's only the Lower Fourth's choir practice, sir," he said, reassuringly. "They'll have finished in a moment." And sure enough, the hymn came to an end and Signor Ruzzi could be heard exclaiming: "Brava, brava, eccellente, bambini, vairy good!"

With a superhuman effort, Mr Culard managed to calm himself down and he turned to the class apologetically. "Forgive my outburst, dear children, but my bats are my prime concern." He got up, walked over to the window and, opening the wire door, banged on the side of the cage. "Now, off you go, my friends, out into the night!" he said.

There was a fluttering of spiky, black wings and all the bats hurtled out of the window, squeaking and flapping, putting several of the girls into near hysterics.

"Calm down, my dears," Mr Culard said, eyeing them intently. "They are lovely creatures. Soon I will give you one to hold. They have soft, furry bodies and tiny white teeth. Delightful animals."

"But, sir," said Simon, who had been quite trans-fixed by this bizarre display, "haven't you lost them for good now they've flown off?"

"I? Lost them? Ah, my young sir, you don't know the way I have with the beasts of the night. They will always return to me. They are specially trained. As you too will be, one day soon, I hope. Trained in biology, that is, so you can pass your exams. And now," he said, looking at the clock, "it is time to end our lesson. I must go on to the Lower Fourths. I hope they will not still be singing hymns. Learn your notes well, my young friends, and we will return to the subject of bats later in the week." And with that he glided slowly from the room clutching his empty cage and leaving the class to reflect on a most extraordinary lesson.

"I think he was really batty!" said Asquith Minor, who'd been dying to get the pun in all lesson. "Don't you think?"

"He was *weird*," said Miles, who still looked shell-shocked after the experience. "As for eating those flies – ugh! But I liked his bats. Certainly makes a change from old Cholmondely."

Susan agreed. "But I didn't like his face. Too spooky."

As everyone left the classroom, Miles sat down in the

teacher's chair and did an imitation of Mr Culard. He put his fingers together. "And now, my dear young friends," he said, "we will study the dinosaur. I happen to have one with me." Tom laughed and Miles got up. "Funny," he said. "Usually when a teacher's been sitting on a chair for half an hour his bum warms up the seat. But that chair's quite cold."

"I can't believe those bats really will go back to him," said Tom. "I bet they're gone for good. That's the last we'll see of them."

But later that night he was proved wrong. After Miles and he had finished secretly watching *Dempsey and Makepiece* on the Sinclair television and turned off the light, Tom couldn't sleep. He couldn't stop thinking about Mr Culard. There was something really evil about him, something deeply wrong. It was as if the man weren't human. Of course no teacher was human, everyone knew that, but Culard... Was it his eyes? They seemed to burn into you like laser guns. Or his skin? No one could really be that pale, surely, and still live – even if he did have Luminosis. Or his teeth? They were so sharp he must have filed them down at the ends. And when he opened his mouth he didn't seem to have any fat, flat teeth at the back like most people – the kind that hurt most when they come loose. Mr Culard had sharp pointed teeth all the way round his jaw, even at the back.

Tom tossed and turned in his bed, unable to drive the image of Mr Culard from his mind. Just thinking of him made him shiver with fear. But however much he wriggled and turned, the sheets and blankets never covered him properly – there was always a draught sneaking in somewhere. He wished he were at home with his nice, puffy duvet to cuddle round him. A

48

sudden wave of homesickness overwhelmed him; he hoped his mum and dad were looking after his hamster properly. What had Mr Culard meant, anyway, when he'd said that hamsters were delicious? Surely he couldn't ever have tasted one! He remembered the funny little munching and chattering noises his hamster made as he picked at seeds through the night. A nice, friendly, homely sound. But as the memory flashed through his mind, he could have sworn he heard a funny chattering noise outside, rather like a hamster. He pulled the sheets over his head, but he could still hear the noise. He got up, opened the window slightly and peered out. The freezing night air hit him like the cold blast from a fridge. There was a full moon which cast a silvery light on the trees in the avenue; even the netball posts shone like lances and far away an owl hooted.

There *was* a squeaking sound, no question of it. And as his eyes accustomed themselves to the darkness, Tom spotted a tiny, fluttering creature whirring about in the blackness. One of Mr Culard's bats! It must be! He craned forward to see it better and watched its flight. First it shimmered in the air as if making up its mind where to go. Then it fluttered along the walls, hovered by the geography master's window – which he had, of course, left open – and flew straight inside.

CHAPTER FOUR

Mr Fox was harassed, as usual. He'd just been discussing the arrangements for the Harvest Festival with his staff and the prospect of the event depressed him.

It had been an informal evening meeting in the Staff Room, one of the only comfortable rooms in the school, with deep armchairs, a carpet on the floor, framed prints on the walls as well as lists of classroom time-tables and rosters, low, cosy lights and even ashtrays for the many secret smokers among them. At one end bubbled a real coffee-making machine which Signor Ruzzi had brought over from Italy — Mr Fox had been presented with a cup as he came in. He gloomily sank into an armchair. He'd have much preferred milky Nescafé himself, but it would be rude to refuse the poisonous, bitter black coffee that Signor Ruzzi made extra strong.

This year Mr Carstairs had undertaken to mastermind the Harvest Festival and he was already present, sitting astride a hard chair turned the wrong way round, his arms crossed over the wooden back. He clutched a brand-new, keen-looking clipboard. Next to him sat Signor Ruzzi, closing his eyes as he sipped blissfully at his coffee; beside him Mrs Grain glared at her watch — four members of staff were late.

"Mr Culard won't be coming," said Mr Fox, putting the untasted cup of coffee by his side, having pretended to take a sip. "And neither will Mr Fritz. He's correcting homework. But where are Mr Roy and Miss Shepherd?"

"Coo—ee! Did I hear my name taken in vain?" The

thin figure of Miss Shepherd, who taught craft and cooking, wafted round the door. "Here I am!" She wiggled her fingers coyly at the other teachers in a coquettish wave. "I'm so sorry I'm late. I was just having a walk round outside in the gloaming, watching the hoar-frost touching the wee tips of the trees' fingers. And saying good night to the dear little birds who are just going to sleep."

Mr Fox felt rather sick, as he always did when confronted by Miss Shepherd. She was thin as a rake, flat as a board and her watery eyes popped out of her head as if an invisible vacuum cleaner pulled at each socket. She had a horrible clean smell about her, as if she had too many baths, and every tremulous extremity of her pale body was tinged with pink blotches – her fingers, her elbows and her nose.

"And I saw Mr Roy who said he was feeling *terribly* ill and was sorry he couldn't come to the meeting, which is such a pity because I know he would make some lovely contributions. It's such an exciting event, isn't it, such a lovely celebration of nature and her bountiful gifts and..."

"Do sit down, you must be tired," said Mr Fox rather tetchily, hoping to make her shut up. "And let's get down to the real nitty-gritty. Now, Carstairs – what are your plans?"

Mr Carstairs coughed and looked around. "This year I really want to make the H.F. *relevant*," he said.

"What's the H.F.?" boomed Mrs Grain, suspiciously. "What's wrong with the words themselves? Harvest Festival. Doesn't take that much longer to say, you know, and I would have thought that you as the English teacher would know how important it is to use the correct words. Sets us off on the right footing."

Mr Carstairs grinned aimiably. "That's what I mean. Relevant. In the past the Harvest Fest" (Mrs Grain winced) "has been far too old-fashioned and fuddy-duddy and not geared to the needs of today. What I'd like to do is to change the name completely to Festaid. How about giving all the produce to the Third World and getting some African musicians to come and play the music? Change the whole service, get in some Maori chants instead of hymns, see if Jimmy Savile and Bob Zeldof – I mean Geldof – couldn't be persuaded to come along. Get the newspapers interested. Have a Harvest marathon, with sponsored runners, on Sunday afternoon. And a sponsored Harvest parachute event. Get some zip into the whole affair."

If Mr Fox's hair could have stood on end after he'd heard Mr Carstairs' plans, it would have done so. (Of course, if Mr Fox's hair *could* have stood on end it would have looked bizarre, about sixty very long strands on one side of his head, nearly reaching the light that swung from the ceiling.) Parachute jumps? The cost of the insurance! Maori chants instead of hymns? The vicar would go bonkers! And what would the old villagers say as they watched the piles of produce being driven past their front doors and off to some godforsaken famine area abroad? They'd go bananas. Luckily he didn't have to say anything because at the mention of African musicians Signor Ruzzi's face had gone bright red. Mr Fox was wondering if the true horror of the evil coffee had finally got to him, but it seemed Carstairs' ideas had been responsible.

"There is *always* the zeep in my music!" he exploded. "Maori chants! Africans! They know nothing of the holy music!" He crossed himself. "Santa Maria, this would be sacrilegious! No bloody good! I hava composed a special joyous Harvest marcha for the occasion, called 'Hurraya for Harvesta'. It is full of laughter but there are quiet parts" – his voice dropped to a hush and his eyes closed blissfully – "full of gratitude. There are sadda parts" – tears came to his eyes as he slowly opened them – "sadda for the end of the year, but most of all there are joyful, hopeful parts" – he perked up and started conducting in mid-air – "hope for a new season next year. A celebration! Full of joy! Maori chants, my feet!"

Mr Carstairs looked thoroughly taken aback by this outburst. He opened his mouth to speak but was interrupted by Miss Shepherd.

"Mr Carstairs, I think your idea is just *wonderful*," she breathed, "and I think you are wonderfully talented to invent it so cleverly. But don't you think it would be a bit – well, violent? And, um, radical? When, in these sadly violent days, perhaps tradition is what we should be after. Tradition and nature. What I suggest is that we get some local people in to play local tunes on lutes and mandolins – under Signor Ruzzi's direction, of course – and garland the whole church with dried branches and fruits from the hedgerows. Maybe we should include square-dancing on the green afterwards – with all the local children joining with our school in a glorious celebration. And let's allow the old folk to pick what they want from the produce – but we should insist that all our gifts are home-grown and healthy. I find it so upsetting to see tins of peas and bags of crisps and boxes of cake-mixes and packets of tea at the altar."

At the mention of packets of tea Mr Fox practically fainted. That was just what he wanted. A nice cup of tea made with a good old-fashioned tea-bag.

"No good getting the local boys and girls doing dances with ours," scoffed Mrs Grain. "Ours would simply be beaten up as they always are. As for the old people choosing their own produce – faugh! Can't you imagine Mrs Pennyweather and Mr Forsyth wrangling over the beetroots? They both adore them. No, far better for me to sort the produce out fairly into baskets and organize the distribution as usual. Why don't we forget all these new ideas and simply have the *Harvest Festival*" – she glared at Mr Carstairs – "just the same as we've always had it?" And, after much argy-bargy and discussion that, of course, is how it all ended up.

Mr Roy was indeed feeling ill. He'd woken that morning with the most terrible headache and when he looked in the mirror he'd been horrified by his deathly pallor. Indeed, he could hardly see himself in the mirror, he felt so grotty. He had a funny itchy rash on his neck and he felt quite woozy when he walked down the corridor. He'd just managed to keep going through lessons but he really wasn't up to facing the annual argument about the Harvest Festival. And yet after an hour's sleep he felt a bit better and managed to totter up to give 2C their last lesson of the day. They could continue with their map-copying, he decided, while he sat at his desk having a quiet snooze, pretending to correct books. But in the event, when he picked up his pen, he was surprised to notice some red marks on his fingers, as if he'd been writing in red ink. He couldn't remember doing anything of the kind. But he'd been feeling so very strange that day. Some virus, presumably. Perhaps it *was* a mistake to sleep with the window quite so wide open in winter. Perhaps he should cosset himself a bit more. He took a handful of sunflower seeds but they didn't really satisfy him. What would make him feel better, he wondered, as he sat, staring into space with nothing to disturb him but the scratching of 2C's pencils on their books? A nice cup of hot milk? Not really. A lightly boiled egg? The idea made him feel ill. A nut cutlet? As his mind fastened on the phrase he found himself repeating the word "cutlet" to himself. Slowly, the picture of the nut cutlet in his mind was replaced by a lamb cutlet, a nice, red, juicy piece of meat, sizzling in a pan. Mmm! Delicious! That was just what he wanted! A great chunk of meat, cooked really rare! He stopped himself. What *was* he thinking of? Was this really Robin Roy thinking? Robin Roy, whose mother had never fed him so much as a single slice of chicken in her lifetime? Robin Roy, a paid-up member of the Vegetarian Society? Robin Roy, who had spent most of his summer holidays campaigning against battery-chicken farming? But oh! He could nearly smell that cutlet now, the delicious aroma of roast meat and the succulent pool of red juices in which it lay...

His reverie was interrupted by Susan who was waving her arm frantically to get his attention.

He pulled himself together. "What's the problem?"

Susan put her arm down and rubbed it. She smiled cheerfully. "Pins and needles. Having it up there so long cut off the blood supply."

Blood? Did she say blood? The mere mention of it made Mr Roy feel dizzy with excitement. What *was* happening to him?

He jerked himself back into reality. "Yes, what is it?" he asked, tartly.

"I've just finished the map which I started yesterday," said Susan. "But when I was checking it just now

I saw it had changed slightly. There seems to be a new country drawn in."

"A new country?" exclaimed Mr Roy. "Oh, Susan, I don't think that's possible. Not unless the European Parliament has been up to some pretty quick work during the night, ha ha! And, knowing the speed at which the European Parliament works, that hardly seems likely!" Everyone giggled gloomily. "Show me. What is all this about?"

"There *is* a new country, sir," squawked Asquith Minor. "Look, in the middle of Romania."

"Yes, look," said Tom, pointing. "I was wondering what that was, too." Probably some country invented yesterday, he thought irritably. No doubt France and Italy would disappear tomorrow. He was glad he hadn't learnt any of them properly the day before.

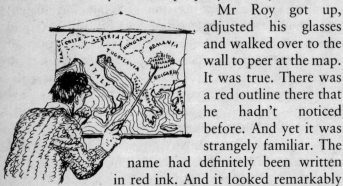

Mr Roy got up, adjusted his glasses and walked over to the wall to peer at the map. It was true. There was a red outline there that he hadn't noticed before. And yet it was strangely familiar. The name had definitely been written in red ink. And it looked remarkably like his own handwriting.

Then everything seemed to become clear to him.

"Oh, yes, of course," he said. "Transylvania. Of *course* that was there yesterday, what on earth are you talking about? Transylvania, Transylvania, everyone knows Transylvania. The most important country in the world."

He returned to his own desk and sat down. He was feeling ever so much better. And yet that was funny. Was he really right about saying that Transylvania was the most important country in the world? Was Transylvania ever a country in its own right at all? He could hardly go back on what he'd said but he had an awful feeling he was wrong. At the same time, there was no doubt that Transylvania *felt* to him like the most important country in the world. He must be ill. He must be hallucinating. He must have caught a brain disease. Or perhaps there was something wrong with his blood. *His blood.* HIS BLOOD. The words pounded into his brain like a ghastly drum-beat. He was caught up by an overwhelming feeling, as if he were being swept away in a howling gale and surrounded by an entire colony of bats flapping and squeaking around him, their wings whirring. He felt as if his brains were being scooped out of his skull with a huge ladle, stirred up with great gobs of madness and evil and then replaced. Then he heard the dark, hypnotic tones of a deep, musty voice.

"I am your Master," it intoned. "You will do everything I ask. You will become as I am, one of the great undead. Soon, the undead will rule the world. You are my servant. You will obey me in all things..."

This was all too much for poor Mr Roy. He fell forward onto his desk and slumped into a dead faint.

"It's all those ridiculous sunflower seeds he eats," declared Mrs Grain at lunch the following day, as she tucked into a vast pile of boiled potatoes. "Thank heavens I've finally managed to persuade him to eat a nice steak today. It's not healthy to eat only vegetables."

The doctor had been summoned to see Mr Roy but

57

Mrs Grain had had to deal with him because Mr Fox stayed firmly in his study with the door shut; after his wife had run away with the doctor after a bad dose of flu, he never trusted himself anywhere near him. As Mr Roy had been so pale the doctor suspected anaemia. He put him on a course of iron pills, recommended a healthy diet and promised to look in the following day.

After lunch Tom was just going out to have a quick game of football on the lawn with Miles, Simon and a few other boys when he bumped into Signor Ruzzi, red-faced and puffing as he came up the drive. The music teacher put a hand on his shoulder and bent double as if he had cramp.

"Buxton, do me the favour. I am coming from the church where I go practise my 'Hurraya for Harvesta' and like a beeg ninny I have left my music in mya room. Run upstairs and bring it down for me, will you? I am alla puffed out. It is just by my bed."

Tom gave an inaudible sigh and turned to go upstairs. As he wouldn't be around to have a say, he'd probably have to be goalkeeper again. What a drag. He started up the stairs, pushing through the throng of kids coming down for the second sitting of lunch.

Mrs Grain had also gone upstairs after the meal, to collect Mr Roy's tray and see how he was. But although every scrap of his lunch had been eaten – the bone from his steak was picked quite clean – Mr Roy was nowhere to be seen. "Mr Roy?" shouted Mrs Grain. "Where are you?"

She went out into the corridor and banged on the lavatory door. "Are you in there?" she demanded. "Are you all right?"

There was no reply but, hearing a noise from Signor Ruzzi's room, she hurried down the corridor and marched in, not noticing Tom who was just about to enter himself. He hung back politely by the door.

"Signor Ruzzi," boomed Mrs Grain, "have you seen...?"

But the only person in the room was Mr Roy himself, who was fiddling intently with the window catch.

"Don't jump!" shouted Mrs Grain, who had done a course as a Samaritan and prided herself on being able to spot suicides. "There's plenty to live for!" And she sprang at the geography master, felling him with a rugby tackle. They both landed on the floor. Mr Roy opened his eyes and stared at Mrs Grain who looked completely dishevelled, shoes off and bun in disarray.

Tom dropped back into the corridor, not wishing to be spotted at this embarrassing moment.

"Mrs Grain!" said Mr Roy. "What are you doing? And why, might I ask, are we in Signor Ruzzi's room?"

"You were trying to commit suicide in here," gasped Mrs Grain, getting up, brushing herself down and holding a hand out to hoick up the invalid. "You just can't deny it. I'll say nothing about it to anyone. But you must promise me never to do that again."

"Suicide?" whimpered Mr Roy. "I must be going mad! Oh, Mrs Grain, you've saved my life!" And he fell into her arms and gave her a huge kiss on the neck. It was rather a violent kiss and Mr Roy couldn't think what had induced him to do it, except that he'd felt a wave of gratitude and a kind of urge that drew him to Mrs Grain's neck. Mrs Grain pushed him away suspiciously and held him at arm's length while rubbing the side of her neck with the other hand. That embrace had rather hurt her. It was more like a bite than a kiss.

"I think you'd better go to your room and lie down," she said in an icy voice. "Come with me." And

Mr Roy allowed himself to be led back to his own bed. What he'd been doing in Signor Ruzzi's room he had no idea, except he had some vague memory of a voice telling him about a window and a lock. He must be delirious. He must be really sick. He clambered thankfully between his sheets and fell into a troubled sleep.

Meanwhile Tom had witnessed the whole scene with growing disbelief. He shook his head in a baffled way as he went to Signor Ruzzi's bedside table and retrieved "Hurray for Harvest". But he couldn't resist looking at the window to see what Mr Roy had been doing there. It was highly unlikely he would have wanted to commit suicide. And yet, it was true, the window catch on the sash had been undone and the window lifted just a few inches. As for that peculiar clinch when Mr Roy had fallen on Mrs Grain's neck, it was more like a vicious attack than a loving kiss of thanks.

As he left the room he felt a violent chill run through him, as if someone had died in there. He hurried downstairs to give the music to Signor Ruzzi.

"Do you think Mr Roy is the type to commit suicide? Or attack someone?"

Mr Roy's bizarre behaviour had triggered off thousands of worrying thoughts in Tom. He and Miles were having their daily wash in neighbouring baths. The communal wash-house was packed with boys in various stages of undress, flicking each other with wet towels, squeezing pieces of soap out of their hands so they landed with a thud on the slippery tiled floor, splashing each other with water and generally shouting and yelling and causing chaos. Simon was sitting in his bath surrounded by a crowd of cronies singing "We All Live in a Yellow Submarine".

"Commit suicide? Mr Roy couldn't commit suicide if you gave him a gun and strapped it to his head. And he could barely attack a . . . a sponge, let alone a person," said Miles, his head a mass of foaming white shampoo. "Why do you ask?"

Tom told him what he'd seen and Miles laughed.

"Good heavens! I didn't realize Roy had it in him," he said, rubbing his scalp vigorously. "He must fancy Mrs Grain! Though how anyone could fancy Mrs Grain is beyond me! They must have been kissing!"

"It didn't seem like kissing to me," said Tom.

He had sometimes seen his mum and dad having a little kiss and a cuddle in front of the telly but it wasn't anything like what Mr Roy had done to Mrs Grain. Perhaps it was something weird and rude – the sort of thing they probably showed in all those films with a 15 rating on them. But he didn't think so somehow. It felt sinister, not loving. However, he didn't want to go on about it to Miles because he might laugh at him. Miles prided himself on being an expert in everything to do with sexual matters. Tom changed the subject.

"Another thing – did you know Mr Culard has an allergy to sunlight – what was it? Mr Carstairs told me. Luminosis?"

Miles burst out laughing. "Luminosis! What's that? Sounds dead phoney. And my father's a doctor so I should know. I'll ask him when I next write. Old Culard certainly suffers from halitosis all right, but Luminosis – stark, staring rubbish if you ask me."

"Things are really funny round here this term," said Tom, standing up and shaking himself before he stepped out of the bath and started to dry himself with a pathetically under-sized towel. "And I mean funny peculiar not funny ha-ha. There's Mr Culard and his

Luminosis, his bats and his fly-eating. There's Mr Roy and that country on his map. And now this thing with Mrs Grain. And there was that bat last night that I saw going into Mr Roy's room. I don't like the look of things at all."

"Rubbish, you're imagining things," said Miles. He put his head under the water and made bubbling noises. Then he emerged, shaking his head like a dog. "You're probably suffering from adolescent delusions. My father says that when you're growing up like we are, all our hormones change and that's why we get spots and sprout hair on our chests and get tired and have funny moods."

Tom didn't think much of this. And he couldn't see how it shed any light on seeing bats or Mr Roy's behaviour. He could just imagine Miles' father, smoothly delivering a speech like that to some wretched patient and then handing over a ginormous bill which would make him feel even worse than when he came in.

"Whatever you say, I think we should keep an eye on things in the future," said Tom.

"The only place I'd like to keep an eye on is the girls' bathroom," muttered Miles as he dunked his head in the water to rinse it. "That'd be a lot more fun."

When they got back to their room they both sat in their dressing gowns on the edge of the bed peering at the television programmes in the paper Miles had smuggled up from the Common Room. He picked at pieces of school cabbage that had got trapped in the brace on his teeth.

"*Newsnight*? Too boring," said Tom, reading out the list of programmes. "*The Verdi Requiem* – 'The Huddersfield Choral Society, founded 150 years ago today, celebrate with a performance of Verdi's choral masterpiece.' No thanks. I don't want to see a lot of epiglottises waggling away at me at this time of night. Or there's *The Lords This Week* — 'Christopher Jones, BBC Parliamentary correspondent, reports on the week's debates in the House of Lords and questions Government...' Yawn, yawn. *The Bob Monkhouse Show*? Can't stand him, can you? It's something about the way he's learnt to smile with his eyes. Never trust a man who smiles with his eyes. Or there's the end of *The Natural World – All Africa Within Us* 'On the banks of the Limpopo River in South Africa, the author Sir Laurens van der Post tells the story of early man's relationship to the animals around him. From Bushman legends he shows how the whole of nature was like a mirror in which man discovered hidden aspects of himself.' Isn't he that boring old twit who's a mate of Prince Charles? What a line-up of programmes. Hardly worth the licence fee. My dreams are more fun than this lot."

And with that they got into their beds and turned out the lights.

It was nearly dawn when Tom was woken by someone frantically shaking his shoulder. He opened his eyes to find Miles standing over him in his pyjamas.

"Go back to bed, I don't want a midnight feast," murmured Tom, drowsily. "I'm tired."

"T–Tom, wake up, wake up," whispered Miles so fast he was stammering. "Please wake up!"

Tom opened one eye. "Leave me alone!" he said tetchily. "I'm knackered. You're probably having an adolescent delusion like you told me about earlier." Even though he was half asleep, he couldn't help feeling one-up as he got his own back. He pressed the light on his digital watch. "For God's sake, it's 5.30 in the morning! Go back to bed. Leave me in peace."

But as he half opened the other eye to look up and make his point, he saw Miles' face was white with terror as he hissed: "There's something *dreadful* outside the window! Quick, quick, look!"

Miles' hands were shaking and he seemed to be almost in tears with fright.

Tom fuzzily got out of bed and staggered over to the window. He craned out, rubbing his eyes. And then he gasped. Because he saw what had frightened Miles so much. There, half-way down the wall outside Signor Ruzzi's room, was Mr Culard, dressed in a black, flapping cloak. And to make things worse, he wasn't just shinning down the drainpipe like an ordinary burglar. He was actually on all fours, *walking down the wall*!

CHAPTER FIVE

"He *couldn't* have been *walking* down the wall," scoffed Susan when, at breakfast the next morning, Tom and Miles reported the morning's events. She'd saved a place for them next to her at the very bottom of the long table, far away from the serving area at the top which was thronged with children.

"You must have had too much cheese on toast last night. Or you were secretly drinking. People can't walk *down* walls. Only *up* walls. Pass the marmalade, will you?"

"Susan, really, I promise you, it did happen," said Tom, desperately. Heavens, she could be irritating. Sometimes she was so condescending and sure of herself it drove him mad. Particularly as Miles deferred to her judgement. But surely she'd believe them. After all, there were two of them trying to persuade her. And there was no question about what they'd seen. In fact they'd been so shaken they'd been unable to get back to sleep and spent the hours of dawn discussing all the possibilities...

"Perhaps he wears special shoes?" Miles had suggested as he lay in bed. "But then why *bother* with special shoes? If he wanted to steal something why not either creep into the school during the night or just shin up the drainpipe like a normal thief?"

"I don't know," Tom had said. "But I'm really frightened, Miles. Do you think he saw us?"

"No, he was staring at the ground ahead of him," Miles had replied, but his voice had wobbled a bit as he said it. "You know, what you were saying yesterday could be right – these bats, the fact he only teaches in the afternoons, Transylvania appearing on Mr Roy's map..."

There was a silence as both of them lay in bed mulling over the same thoughts. There was no sound from outside – just the deadly silence of an autumn dawn; even the birds seemed to find it too cold to get up from their warm nests. A faint, fishy-grey light glittered through the thin curtains, giving every object in the room the dead look of uncleaned silver.

"You don't think..." said Tom.

"Think what?" said Miles, nervously.

"Well, do you remember what Mr Fritz was saying about his...holidays?" he suggested, ambiguously. He didn't want Miles to think he was silly. There was a long silence from Miles' bed. Then: "It's this Luminosis that worries me – not liking sunlight," said Miles finally, equally unwilling to commit himself.

"And what was all that about Transylvania in Mr Roy's lesson? And these bats of Mr Culard's..."

"And the way he ate those flies. He can't be like ordinary people," added Miles.

"Do you really think that he could be a...?" said Tom, at last.

"Could be what?" whispered Miles, cautiously.

"A... a... vampire." As he spoke the unspeakable, Tom felt himself burst out in goose-pimples.

"But why would a vampire want to come to Burlap Hall?" asked Miles, anxiously.

"It's a big school," said Tom. "There are 350 people here. We're all miles from anywhere. We're not likely to be believed if we tell anyone. We're young and juicy."

At the word "juicy" Miles flinched. "But I thought

vampires only liked young female virgins," he said hopefully.

"There are plenty here," said Tom, "and anyway, that's just in films, an excuse to get lots of sexy ladies in ripped blouses on the screen. In real life vampires will bite anything, as long as it's full of blood, don't you think?"

"But what can we do about it?" said Miles. "Mr Roy must have been got at already and as Mr Culard was walking down from Signor Ruzzi's room, he'll probably be the next to show symptoms."

"First we've got to get more evidence," Tom replied thoughtfully, "otherwise no one's going to believe us."

"Susan will," said Miles, as he heard the bell ringing. He put one leg tentatively out of bed and then reached for his socks.

But Susan had been totally sceptical and now, as she chomped on a piece of rubbery toast, she shook her head vigorously.

"He's a biology teacher, after all. Of course he's got animals for us to study. Why not bats? It makes a change."

"I seem to remember some law about bats," said Tom, thoughtfully, shaking a few limp cornflakes into his bowl. "Didn't old Cholmondely tell us that it was illegal to kill or even possess bats because they were in danger of becoming extinct? How can Mr Culard be allowed to own these bats? And anyway, don't bats live in caves and hollow trees? Not in cages, surely."

"They do in London Zoo," said Miles. "I've seen them hanging there." And he did a quick impression of a bat by pursing his lips, closing his eyes and clasping his hands above his head as if hanging in a trance.

"They hang upside-down, you wally," said Tom, "and anyway, in London Zoo they don't live in cages, they have a special bat-like environment constructed for them so they're fooled into *thinking* they're living in a cave."

"Environment? That's a long word for you to use — it's got more than three syllables," teased Susan, having a sip of tea, "and couldn't you think of another word that didn't have the word 'men' in it?"

"Don't change the subject," said Tom, seriously, "I'm frightened, I mean it."

Susan looked at him pityingly. "You really are pathetic," she said. "Anyway, why would he call himself a weird name like Mr Culard, if he were a vampire trying to blend in with the scenery? He'd call himself an ordinary name like Smith. Mr A. Culard," she added, reflectively. "Incidentally, I wonder what the A stands for?" She picked up the remains of her toast but, just as she was about to pop it into her mouth, a faraway look came into her eyes and she went pale.

"Mr A. Culard," she breathed in a low, nervous voice. "Jesus Christ! Sorry, I mean, Holy Mary! It's an anagram! A-C-U-L-A-R-D spells Dracula! So Mr Culard is really Count Dracula!"

At this new piece of evidence, panic gripped Tom. Suddenly he rather wished Susan *hadn't* believed them. His ankles had gone tense and dead as if he were rooted to the spot, his heart started pounding and his mouth went dry. He remembered having exactly the same feeling when he was about two years old and he'd been taken to the seaside to go paddling for the first time. At the unfamiliar feeling of the waves trickling over his feet, he'd stood rigid, his bucket and spade clutched in his hand, and burst into terrified tears.

"We've got another biology lesson today," whispered Susan. "Let's test him out on a few things. Just to make sure. We'll ask him about the bats. Shouldn't they be hibernating now, anyway? How come his are full of beans? We'll see if he goes to church – vampires hate churches. Let's ask him if he's coming to the Harvest Festival on Sunday. Vampires don't have reflections, either. Anyone got a mirror? And they don't cast shadows... And there's always the garlic angle. I'll see if I can pinch some from the kitchens. Let's put him through his paces in class. But I think you might be right. It all starts fitting into a pattern."

Once they had all discussed it together, however, Tom felt more confident. They'd worked out a plan of questioning in class and as he sat at his desk later that afternoon waiting for Mr Culard to come in, his heart pounded with a mixture of excitement and fear at the prospect of the lesson. Today Mr Culard was giving notes on the basic biology of bats. He stood in front of the class reading from a long, dirty piece of paper.

"'Bats are the only flying mammals and like other mammals they have fur, are very intelligent, suck – I mean suckle – their young and have a complex social life,'" he droned in his hypnotic voice. "'Their wings are formed of skin supported by arms and elongated fingers. They can live up to thirty years.'

"How do bats see in the dark, you will be asking? I will tell you. 'They are not blind but their most highly developed sense is that of hearing. They use a form of sonar for obstacle avoidance and for locating food. There are fifteen different types of bat in Britain.' Take this list down, please."

He took a deep, rasping breath, as if he were

inhaling centuries of dust, and began reciting slowly: "'Noctule, Leisler's bat, Serotine, Barbastelle, Brown long-eared bat, Grey long-eared bat, Pipistrelle, Mouse-eared bat, Natterer's bat, Daubenton's bat, Whiskered bat, Brandt's bat, Bechstein's bat, Greater Horseshoe bat and last, but not least, Lesser Horseshoe bat.'"

This was a cue for Susan; her arm shot up. "Sir, what about Vampire bats?" she asked.

Tom and Miles held their breath. Mr Culard looked at her slowly, his huge, blood-shot eyes boring in on her like red-hot rays. His head sank into his great, dark shoulders as if he were peering out from behind a large, black rock, and he licked his red lips in a repulsively voluptuous way. Tom could hear his slimy, slug-like tongue slapping round his mouth.

"Vampire bats," he repeated ponderously, sucking over the words as if they were boiled sweets. "Are you interested in Vampire bats, my dear? I can tell you a lot about Vampire bats, but as they are not an English species we will not be studying them for the exams. They are small — around three and a half inches in length — and are reputed to suck the blood from mammals... However, if you want to hear more about Vampire bats, I will be happy to give you special, private classes in the evenings. Tell me your name, my dear," he added, pulling a black pen from his greasy pocket, "and we will come to an — how would you call it? — an arrangement."

Susan looked terrified. "Oh, thanks a lot, sir, but I've got so much on at the moment that I don't think I've got time to study any more. I don't want to put you out. And I haven't got any free periods. None at all."

"What a very great pity," said Mr Culard, slowly,

but he still didn't put his pen away. "Your question interests me and I may be able to make some *special notes* which you may like to read over for pleasure. Let me have your name, anyway."

"My name? Um, Susan, er, Susan...Sanders," said Susan, inventing a surname.

"Your name's not Susan Sanders," squawked Asquith Minor. "It's Susan..."

"That's right, I should know, I share a room with you," added Rosemary in her special "tell-tale" voice.

"It *is* Sanders," said Susan, angrily, turning round to face Asquith Minor as she racked her brain for an excuse. "My mother remarried and my stepfather has adopted me and I've changed my name and I've taken my mother's maiden name on principle, which is, incidentally, my aunt's middle name because..."

"Susan Sanders," said Mr Culard, smiling intimately at her, licking the tip of his pen and making some notes on a piece of paper. "I shall check the correct spelling with Mr Fox. But I shall remember you because of your delightful red hair. I love the colour red." He finished his notes with a flourish and returned the pen to his pocket. "Any more questions?" he asked.

Miles bravely put up his hand. "Sir, last term we were told it was illegal to possess bats as they are a protected species. How come you own your bats?"

"I have a special licence," said Mr Culard with a deep-seated chuckle that sounded, to Tom's fevered imagination, like rivers of blood gurgling into a sewer. "A very special licence from the University of Bistrita. Perhaps you would like to see the certificate one night?" Miles shuddered. "I love bats, and I would never do anything to harm them. I would rather harm the people who harm the bats. I think they deserve to be PUNISHED!" he added, his voice suddenly turning into a roar of rage. He glared at the class, his red lips drawn back over his teeth like a wild animal. Tom noticed that two of his side teeth were distinctly longer and more pointed than the rest.

"However," he added, in a softer voice, recovering himself, "that is neither here nor there. I will now draw a bat on the board and I would like you to copy it into your notebooks."

While his back was turned it was Tom's chance to produce the small pocket mirror that Susan had provided. He turned it to face Mr Culard's broad, black back and craned his neck over the glass to see if the teacher had a reflection. Unfortunately all he could see was a lock of his own hair. As he twisted and turned, he moved the mirror this way and that and it caught a fading ray of sunlight from outside which danced on the ceiling, the walls, the desk and finally flickered briefly on Mr Culard's coat.

As it rested between his huge, bony shoulders, Mr Culard gave a sudden groan of pain and whirled round. Tom managed to hide the mirror under his hand, his heart pounding.

"Did someone throw a dart at me?" Mr Culard roared at the class menacingly.

Everyone shook their heads vigorously. Mr Culard didn't turn back to the board but eyed the pupils dangerously. "Something happened just then. I don't want it to happen again." His voice was cold as ice, glittering with precision and menace.

Tom turned his eyes surreptitiously to Susan and saw her nodding quietly at him. "Sunlight," she mouthed.

The bell rang before Mr Culard could go any further but he held up his hand for quiet.

"For homework over the weekend I want you to learn these notes and also some others I will distribute to you. In addition, I would like you to perfect the art of drawing a bat, " he said. "I will not be seeing you until Monday and I will test you all then."

Tom spoke up bravely. "Oh, Mr Culard, sir, surely we'll be seeing you at the Harvest Festival on Sunday? It's going to be such a special occasion in the church."

"No, Buxton, I have other things to do," replied Mr Culard, coldly. "And I never go to church. I disapprove of the Christian religion. There is only one religion that encompasses all things...but no matter. Soon you will learn of it. Maybe when you grow up. *If* you grow up," he added, with a ghastly chuckle, spitting flecks of grey saliva onto the floor in his glee.

"Of course we'll grow up," said Asquith Minor indignantly. "What do you mean, sir?"

"I meant it metaphorically," said Mr Culard, "because this seems a particularly silly and frivolous class. But I am certain that my remarks will not go unheeded in some quarters." And it seemed to Tom as if he were looking directly at him.

The Sunday of the Harvest Festival was one of those mellow autumn days that come only on special occasions – usually when one has planned to spend all day doing something indoors. Outside the church, golden leaves dripped off the trees in the warm October breeze, circling slowly down to add to the rich carpet of brown, yellow and orange below. The moss growing round the church door was on the turn as well, giving a gilded look to the whole building as it stood out in silhouette against a glorious chill-blue sky. It wasn't hot, but the air gave out a faint, faraway heat like a slowly cooling fire.

Inside, the church was cold but glowing as the wan sun pressed its way through the windows and fell onto the altar, surrounded by great bunches of dried flowers arranged by Miss Shepherd. In front of the pulpit were huge baskets of produce — cauliflowers, tomatoes, beans, potatoes — and occasionally, peeping out from underneath, the odd can of peas, bag of white flour or packet of sausages that Miss Shepherd had unsuccessfully tried to hide from view.

In the centre of all this glowing tranquillity Mr Carstairs paced up and down the aisle, his clipboard gripped in his hand.

"Where in Heaven's name is Signor Ruzzi?" he demanded impatiently of no one in particular — though of course he might have been addressing God. He could hear the pupils slowly gathering outside the church but he was reluctant to let them in because his plan had been for Ruzzi to be there half an hour before the service started, playing the organ softly — a nice dramatic touch. But Ruzzi hadn't turned up. After all that wretched fuss he'd made about his flipping organ music, felt Carstairs, he could at the very least have been on time.

Just then, to his relief, he noticed the bulky silhouette of the music master lurking in the church entrance.

"Come on in, hurry up, you're late," he hissed, hurrying down the aisle towards him. "Get playing!"

But, approaching the stone lobby by the church door, he noticed that Signor Ruzzi seemed to be struggling with himself. He would walk forwards into the church, and then fall back with an irritated grunt, knocking against the list of weekly flower arrangers and times of services that hung by the oak door. Then he made another attempt to push through, and staggered back again, this time onto a pile of hymn books.

"A thousand apologies, Mr Carstairs," gasped Signor Ruzzi, picking himself up and gingerly reorganizing the pile of books. "I oversleep, I am not feeling myself. I have thees terrible rash on my neck and now I am overcome with feelings... Mama Mia...what is wrong with theesa church, there is a terrible attamossapher in here. I am feeling faint when I come in, perhaps someone has been poleeshing the pews with the horrible poleesh maybe and I am allergica..."

"Oh, for heaven's sake, pull yourself together, man," snapped Mr Carstairs, pulling him in violently. "The service only lasts an hour, then you can go to bed. Good God, everyone seems to be ill round here. You should take more exercise, you know. I keep telling you you should drink less coffee, cut out fats and come on our runs. Good heavens, you look terrible!"

For when he finally saw him clearly, having half dragged him up the aisle into a patch of watery sunlight, he could see that Signor Ruzzi was not only deathly pale but unshaven as well and his collar was pulled away from his neck showing livid spots on one side. For a moment he was going to comment further but he thought it best to say nothing in case it worried Signor Ruzzi even more.

"Now you sit down at the organ and start playing and I'll get everyone in."

Mr Carstairs then sprinted to the door and flung it wide open to greet Mr Fox who stood smiling in his gown, accompanied by Miss Shepherd. Behind them the pupils followed, taking their places in the pews. But still no music. What a shambles, he thought. Everything was going wrong with this Harvest Festival. He'd never volunteer to do it again.

"Get playing, man!" he whispered as he passed Signor Ruzzi. But on his organ seat the music master seemed turned to stone. He stared ahead at the sheet of music in front  of him – a mass of cheerful quavers and staccato notes under the title "Hurray for Harvest".

Eventually Signor Ruzzi sighed deeply, put his hands on the keyboard and started to play. The organ notes boomed out deep and drear, like a dirge. And as he continued, the tune sounded familiarly gloomy, the notes booming out like a death-knell.

"That's the Funeral March!" whispered Tom to Miles, as they took their places in the pew; he recognized it from the funeral of his carrot-nosed aunt.

A minor uproar was now occurring around the organ, with the music getting louder and louder and more and more gloomy and Mr Carstairs arguing with Signor Ruzzi and trying to persuade him to stop. Eventually Miss Shepherd agreed to take over and Carstairs hurried Signor Ruzzi from the church.

"Go and get some sleep, you'll feel better later," he said, as kindly as he could, but between clenched teeth. Inside he was fuming. The Maori chants and the African musicians would have worked *far* better. However, taken all in all, the service finally worked out quite well. True, there was rather a lot of whispering, because so many of the teachers were absent – Mrs Grain seemed to have caught Mr Roy's ailment and was spending time in bed – but Miss Shepherd played

Signor Ruzzi's "Hurray for Harvest" with great gusto, and the pensioners sang out energetically as they peered urgently at the baskets of produce to see which one looked the most promising. The vicar was on top form and vigorously blessed all the gifts and when everyone filtered out after the service it was agreed that the occasion had gone splendidly.

It was only Tom and the others who felt deeply worried by the whole service. While everyone else tittered as Signor Ruzzi was ushered from the church, Tom felt sick with fear and anxiety. Never a great one for hymns or psalms, he found he couldn't sing a note his throat was so dry. When he knelt down to pray he could only say the Lord's Prayer in a hoarse whisper. And during the sermon, which was all about God's harvest, Tom could only think about Mr Culard walking down the wall from Signor Ruzzi's room. God only knew what he had done to the poor man. Try as he might to wrench his mind away from the subject, it seemed to be pinned to the topic, as immovable as the north needle on a compass. He tried to think of his parents, his hair, *Top of the Pops*, the last episode of *EastEnders* – all in vain. His brain was stuck on the subject of vampires whether he liked it or not.

Meanwhile Mrs Grain had finally got out of bed to organize the delivery of the baskets to the needy parishioners. She certainly felt terrible and her eyesight seemed to be fading – she could hardly see herself in the mirror that morning and hoped she wasn't looking scruffy – but she had heard how Signor Ruzzi had behaved earlier on and was determined to show him that English women were made of sterner stuff. *She* could certainly cope, however ill she was feeling.

When she arrived, most of the pupils were wandering back to Burlap Hall; only the form monitors remained to deliver the baskets. But Mr Fritz, who had witnessed the day's events with a puzzled frown, hung around to keep an eye on Mrs Grain, who looked far from well; and Susan also hovered about near Tom.

"Slip this into the basket Mrs Grain carries and see what happens," she whispered tucking a round, dry object into his hand.

Tom looked down and saw it was a bulb of garlic. "What's that for?" he asked.

"Vampires hate garlic – she'll probably freak out if she's anywhere near it," said Susan. "I've got to rush back for lessons, now. But good luck!"

Tom watched her go with a twinge of loneliness. He didn't like doing things like this all on his own. Even Susan would be better than no one. Still, he sauntered over to the baskets and hung about looking interested as Mrs Grain sketched out her plan in a faint voice. She doled out the baskets to the monitors and, while her back was turned, Tom popped the bulb of garlic into one of them.

"This one's for Mrs Pennyweather, at number 5, The Almhouses," she said, getting to the end of the list and handing the basket to Tom. Heavens, she felt so dizzy in the sunlight. "And this one is for Mr Forsyth, at number 4," she added, picking up the second to last basket and giving it to a spotty girl in 1A. "And this last one is for the Misses Potter, at number..." She reached down, picked up the basket which contained the garlic – and then let it drop with a howl. "Hell and demons!" she screeched. "My hand, my hand!" Looking down she saw it was scorched and bloody as if she'd put it on a hotplate. But the shock didn't last for long because she felt a great wind swirling around her, and she seemed to be surrounded by a host of black, flapping sour-smelling objects, squeaking like mice. A deep, musty voice spoke to her through what seemed to be a cloud of fog.

"I am your Master," it intoned. "You will do everything I ask. You will become as I am, one of the great undead. Soon the undead will rule the world. You are my servant. You will obey me in all things."

Tom had hurried away in such a panic he didn't see Mrs Grain falling to the ground in a sickening swoon and Mr Fritz hurrying to attend to her, gathering up the contents of the spilled basket. He noticed the garlic and, with a troubled look, slipped it into his pocket; he also took a bag of flour. His suits were so ill-made and baggy that a few items like garlic and flour in one of the pockets made no difference at all to the line of the jacket.

Tom was completely shaken. He had hardly been able to stagger down to the village with his basket because his knees had turned to jelly. Everything seemed to be moving so fast; if Mr Culard were a vampire he was certainly working quickly. Life at Burlap Hall, never a pleasant affair, was at least always predictable; now it was getting out of control. So when Mrs Pennyweather had asked him in for a cup of tea he was surprised to find himself accepting, because normally he wouldn't go anywhere near Mrs Pennyweather, a hag-like old woman with hair on her chin and a smell of stale urine clinging to her person.

He sat well away from her in her poky sitting room, trying to sip the tea from the cup without actually touching the sides as they were covered with scabby, brown stains.

He knew he should ask her about her arthritis or her corns — all old people love being asked about their health he had discovered — but he couldn't bring himself to listen to a dismal speech about her doctor and the operations she either had had or was about to have. He thought of saying "Cold weather we're having for the time of year," like some people did, but in fact the sort of weather they were having was just about normal for the time of year. There was nothing unusual about it at all. He couldn't ask her about the Harvest Festival because she hadn't been able to get to it — no doubt because of her arthritis — which took Tom back to the first subject he'd already rejected. Finally a thought struck him.

"Do you know where Mr Culard lives in the village?" he asked.

"Mr Culard? Mr Culard? Never heard of him!" cackled Mrs Pennyweather, smacking her lips. "There's no one living in the village who hasn't lived here fifty years or more!"

"He's a teacher at the school, tall, wears black, apparently he's taken these rooms round here," said Tom, speaking louder so she didn't miss a word.

"Taken beetroots? He's taken the beetroots? I particularly asked Mrs Grain..."

"No, this man, Mr Culard, he's taken *these rooms* in the village," said Tom, loudly.

"No strangers living in this village nor any village

within miles around to my certain knowledge," said Mrs Pennyweather. "And I know everything that's going on in this village, inside and out. Any beetroots in that basket, young man? I love beetroots."

"No, but I'll get some for you from the school vegetable garden if you want," said Tom, leaning forward urgently. "Is there anything odd going on around here, would you say? Any, er, bats?"

"Any beets? I thought you told me there were none. Don't lie to me, young man. I'll be telling Mr Fox of you, if you don't watch it!"

"*Bats*, not beets," said Tom, exasperated. "Is there anything strange going on round here?"

"Strange, that I'll say," said Mrs Pennyweather. A drip of tea hung on the end of one of the hairs on her chin, about to plop into her dirty skirt. "Bats all over the place. Wrong time of year, too. Ought to be hibernating. And there are these foxes at night, barking and howling. Can't sleep. They sound like wolves."

After his sickly cup of tea and the worrying information given him by Mrs Pennyweather, Tom returned to school plunged in gloom and anxiety.

What on earth were they going to do? How could he, Tom Buxton, thirteen years old, son of Mr and Mrs Buxton, London, England, have a hope against Mr Culard, better known as Count Dracula, heaven knows how old but probably centuries, son of Count and Countess Dracula (presumably) of Dracula Castle, Transylvania? Tom was not only half his size and probably a fraction of his age, but Mr Culard possessed magical vampire style powers and he, Tom, possessed none. Unless you could call being able to loop the loop with a yo-yo, or make a face like a monkey or pull a coin from someone's ear, powers. At least Miles and Susan felt the same way, but none of them knew the first thing about vampires except that they had long teeth and sucked blood and were often on telly at 12.05 a.m. He'd never been allowed up that late except once on New Year's Eve when he'd blown it by falling fast asleep at five to twelve.

He felt as if he were living in a nightmare from which he couldn't wake up. The fact that the others weren't around because they were finishing the scripture lesson he'd been allowed to miss because of his basket-distributing duties made him feel even more unhappy and lonely.

He wandered into the Common Room and tried to read a paper. But he couldn't concentrate. He leaned out of the window for a breath of fresh air – but immediately saw the wall down which Mr Culard had walked. When his watch suddenly squeaked out – he had a habit of setting the alarm to go off every hour to mark the end of each lesson – he jumped, thinking it was the squeaking of a bat. He had the horrible feeling that Mr Culard was there in the room with him, watching him; he found himself going up to the curtains and flicking them away from the walls with a sudden movement, half hoping to catch him hiding.

Eventually he could stand it no longer. He went to the desk and got out a piece of paper. He knew he was being pathetic and cowardly and everything he shouldn't be, but he was desperate.

He sat down and started a letter.

Dear Mum and Dad,
        Please, please come and take me away from here. I am so miserable and frightened I don't

know what to do. I know you'll think this is ridiculous but I think all the teachers are turning into vampires. Soon we will all be vampires if I don't get away. Please take my letter seriously, I promise you I'm not joking. Please, please come as soon as possible.

All my love,

Tom

PS. Please come as soon as possible.

CHAPTER SIX

Some time later Tom still hadn't heard from his parents. Why hadn't they written or at least rung him up? They were usually so understanding. Surely...? Surely not. It couldn't be that Mr Culard had somehow intercepted the letter? He couldn't bear to think of such a thing. Perhaps he should have posted it himself instead of leaving it on the hall table, where the letters were usually left for Mr Fox to take to the post office.

The teachers who had been ill were on the mend — but as they recovered so they became increasingly unkempt. Mrs Grain, normally buxom and immaculate, revealed ladders in her lisle stockings, her shoes were scuffed and ragged, as if she'd been wandering about in bushes, her bun was coming adrift and she made no effort to put it back neatly. Although she never wore lipstick, priding herself on a plain, scrubbed complexion, her lips seemed redder than before.

Mr Roy had changed from a wimpy vegetarian into a great meat-eater, often rubbing his stomach before mealtimes and giving an embarrassingly loud growl as he entered the dining room, muttering: "Meat! Meat! Will it be chops today? Or steak? Or mince?" He had changed his special subject that term from Europe to Middle-Europe and he took pleasure in showing maps of Romania to the class, paying great detail to towns like Cluj, Fundu and Veresti with particular attention on the Borgo Pass in the Carpathian mountains which bordered Transylvania. He, too, had lost his dapper appearance and was starting to remind Tom of an old wino he had once discovered squatting at the end of their garden in a pool of beer.

As for Signor Ruzzi, he seemed to be heading for a nervous breakdown. In music lessons he would start playing a light-hearted piece and explain what it meant. Twiddle-twiddle, he would go on the piano, and then turn coyly to the class. "You hear it? The fawn? Peepeeng shyly from behind a tree? That is what Schumann wanted us to hear, the animals of the forest, playing and dancing in the spring sunshine." Plunk! he'd go on the piano after a few more chords. "Could that be a leetle frog, popping shyly from the pond?" Then the chords would get gloomier and darker – "And now the thunderstorm, the night is falleeng, all the animals are running for cover!" There'd be a lot of scales, to signify the animals racing for their burrows...

All this was normal in Signor Ruzzi's music lessons, just as boring as usual, thought Tom. But since his illness Signor Ruzzi's ideas had become a lot more bizarre. He would get to the thunderstorm bit and then go on, improvising as he went, the music getting faster and more furious. "You can hear the winds are howling...now, the full moon seengs out over the land...and what is that sound? Leesten, perhaps the squeaking of a bat, darting through the darkness...and hark! the wolves," he'd add, as he played a high, howling chord. "Ah, the children of the night! What music theya make!"

The only teachers who seemed to be normal were Mr Carstairs, Miss Shepherd, Mr Fox and Mr Fritz – and even he was more forgetful and anxious than usual, worrying and fussing about every tiny detail.

"We ought to ask him about vampires," said Miles, a couple of days after they'd discussed it all with Susan.

"He obviously knows all about them. If there *is* something funny going on, he'll be able to help."

"You don't think he knows *too* much about them, do you?" suggested Susan, nervously. "I find it — I don't know — a bit suspicious that he's just come back from Romania and now all this is happening. Wouldn't it be better to go to Mr Carstairs?"

"He'd just tell us what great imaginations we'd got and why didn't we write a story about it," said Tom. "But I know what you mean. The thing is — who else could we confide in? Miss Shepherd's off her trolley, Mr Fox wouldn't bother to listen...Mr Fritz is very approachable."

"Perhaps we should play it by ear then," said Miles.

"You mean go in and tell him we're worried about things in general? I can't see how we can tell him and not tell him."

"Let's mention vampires to him and see what his reaction is," said Tom. "Then we can tell him more if we feel like it."

They all agreed and during their next free period they found Mr Fritz in his study and asked if they could talk to him.

"Of course, of course," he said, gesturing for them to sit down. His room was a mass of papers, maps, test tubes, piles of iron filings, bottles of gases and liquids. There was a weird smell of chemicals about the place, mingled with the sickly reek of his pipe. As there was nowhere to sit, Tom and Miles settled cross-legged on the floor, while Susan perched on the end of the bed.

"What's your problem?" beamed Mr Fritz. "Want to know why limewater turns cloudy when carbon dioxide is passed through it? Or whether copper carbonate loses or gains mass when heated? Let me hear what's puzzling you. Perhaps I haven't explained something properly?"

"Sir, it's not really to do with science," said Tom, looking up at him.

Mr Fritz looked so relaxed, lounging in his big leather chair and puffing at his pipe, that Tom hardly liked to broach the subject of vampires. The science teacher had looked worried when they found him and seemed so relieved at the prospect of a chat to them, that Tom felt ashamed of badgering him.

"We wondered..." Tom said, then stopped.

"Yes?" said Mr Fritz, helpfully. He gave an encouraging grin and breathed out a ring of smoke. "Don't be shy. There's nothing wrong with not understanding something. I'm always here to explain. Just fire away."

"It's about...vampires," said Tom at last.

None of them were prepared for Mr Fritz's reaction. He seemed to shoot up out of his chair as if he were being launched at Cape Canaveral. His pipe flew out of his hand, and his face went the colour of uncooked pastry. When he had come down to earth, his hands shook slightly as he reached for his pipe.

But then he recoverd himself slightly. He packed his pipe tighter and took a long suck at it. He leant back in his chair and closed his eyes. "Yes?" he said, almost curtly. "What do you want to know? I know all children find vampires amusing, but I'm afraid I don't, so I'm not prepared to have a good laugh about them, if that's what you're after."

"But, sir, we don't find them funny either," exploded Miles. "We're all *terrified*!"

"Sir, we think that Mr Culard is Dracula," said Susan, getting it out at last. "His name is an anagram.

He keeps bats."

Mr Fritz's eyes glittered. "This is fascinating," he breathed. "A. Culard. Dracula. Tell me – what else do you know?"

They all hesitated. They'd agreed to wait for Mr Fritz's reaction before revealing any of their other suspicions, but they hadn't discussed what sort of reaction they would deem favourable. True, he'd seemed surprised and horrified – but perhaps that was because he *was* a vampire and was surprised and horrified that they'd found him out. Why was Mr Fritz so interested after all? Wasn't that rather strange in itself? Ordinary teachers would pooh-pooh ideas about vampires. Perhaps Mr Fritz had been bitten by a vampire on holiday in Romania and had brought Mr Culard back with him...

"We don't know a lot," said Tom, cagily. "We thought you might be able to shed some light on the situation."

He was staring intently at the ground by Mr Fritz's legs to work out whether he cast a shadow. But it was all rather dark and gloomy round there and he couldn't really see.

As Mr Fritz removed his pipe from his mouth, Tom was relieved to see his teeth seemed just the same length as usual. That was something. "Yes, I must say, this Luminosis is rather odd, isn't it?" he said. "It's not something I have ever come across in my studies. Talking of Luminosis, it's dark isn't it? Let's turn on the light." He reached over to his lamp and snapped it on. To Tom's relief his arm cast a definite shadow on the table. "But I don't think we ought to jump to conclusions, do you? I must say I've been a bit worried about this so-called bug that seems to be going around. I find it odd that Mr Roy has suddenly started to eat meat. And it was strange that Mrs Grain let her basket drop, wasn't it? I found a piece of garlic inside it, by the way. Could be the reason, as vampires hate garlic. And I heard today that Miss Shepherd is unwell."

"We thought that everyone being unwell was because they'd been bitten by Mr Culard and turned into vampires," said Susan.

Tom thought she was being far too open with Mr Fritz and interrupted. "But of course it may just be a dose of flu," he said. "It's probably nothing."

Mr Fritz seemed to be thinking hard. Try as he might, Tom couldn't make out whether he was mulling over the facts in a helpful way, or whether he was deep in the middle of dreaming up some horrible scheme to shut them up.

"I must admit I'm not too sure about this," said Mr Fritz, thoughtfully. "But what I am sure of is that you mustn't tell anyone else about it. Don't breathe a word to a soul."

Tom felt more uneasy than ever. When he'd seen the shadow he was sure Mr Fritz wasn't a vampire, but now he'd told them not to say anything to anyone else, he felt fairly certain he *was* one. It was very sinister.

"What we need is hard evidence. Proof," said Mr Fritz, sucking intently on his pipe. "It would be terrible to make a mistake about all this. If this were a scientific experiment, would there be any possibility of proof? None at all."

Tom felt even more alarmed. It reminded him of those bits in murder stories where the detective confronts the murderer with the evidence – usually on a cliff-top – and the murderer smiles cunningly and says, "Be that as it may, you have no proof! No one would believe you!" He shivered. But he didn't feel cold. Probably because of Mr Fritz's jolly log fire crackling away in the grate. And then Tom became confused again. Vampires detest fires. Surely a real vampire wouldn't have a blazing log fire in his room? But Mr Fritz was talking. "Let us approach this scientifically. We will do a little experiment. I took the opportunity, after the Harvest Festival, to retrieve this bag of flour from a basket – it had been blessed by the vicar. I had been hoping to find a way of using it myself to get some proof. But now I think about it, why don't you suggest Miss Shepherd uses it at her next cookery class? Then report to me what happens. When we meet again we'll discuss the matter further."

With this, he rose from his chair, rummaged about behind a pile of bags of crystals and books, and produced the bag of flour he had so carefully filched from the Harvest Festival basket. He handed it over to Susan carefully, as if it were a crown jewel. But even at this tense juncture Susan remembered her feminist principles.

"Come on, just because I'm a girl doesn't mean I'm the only one here who does cooking classes," said Susan, folding her hands obstinately in her lap. "Give it to one of the boys."

Tom sighed and took it. "All right, all right," he said. "You know he just meant to be polite."

"Not meant," snapped Susan, tartly. "Woment."

Outside Mr Fritz's door they compared notes. "I thought he was OK," said Susan, warily. "I saw his reflection in his bedside mirror."

"I don't know if we did the right thing," said Miles. "The thing is, even the nicest teachers are so weird, none of them are like ordinary people."

"Did you know there's a phrase which goes 'Those who can, do; those who can't, teach?'" said Tom.

"And those who teach are all extremely weird," added Miles. "But I've got to go or I'll be late for Chess Club. See you."

Susan walked along the corridor with Tom. They could hear the sounds of grunts and gasps from one of the classes doing gym below, the faraway tinkling of a piano lesson and the drone of a teacher loudly giving out notes to pupils in a neighbouring classroom.

"He casts a shadow. He had a fire burning. He might be OK," said Tom, doubtfully. There was a pause.

"I wish I wasn't at this horrible school," said Susan. "If I'd gone to school in the States none of this would have happened to me. We don't have vampires in the States, you know. They're purely European."

"Then it's funny that the great vampire actor, Vincent Price, happens to be American," said Tom defensively, who was rather hurt by this outburst.

"We have the best actors," said Susan, "but no vampires. You have the vampires but no actors. At least none worth writing home about."

"Oh, thanks," said Tom, angrily. "Just forget about Laurence Olivier, Richard Burton, John Hurt, Richard Harris, Peter O'Toole..." He felt really fed up with Susan. Things were difficult enough without rowing about which country had the best actors. "I bet there are vampires in America, anyway."

"Oh, Tom, I'm sorry." Susan stopped in the corridor and turned her head away from him. "I'm just worried sick." And she put up a hand to her face as if to brush away a tear. "I just wish I were somewhere else. I find it all so frightening. Don't you?"

"Yes, I do," said Tom, coming over and giving her a

comforting pat on the back. "I'm scared stiff. I even wrote to my parents the other day asking them to take me away. Don't tell Miles," he added hastily. Miles would think he was being pathetic.

"Did you?" Susan turned round, cheered up by the news. "I was thinking of sending my parents a similar letter by Diplomatic Bag."

"What's Diplomatic Bag?" asked Tom as they both continued down the stairs, now Susan had recovered.

"It's a special method of post to send letters to diplomats. So they can tell each other secrets and things without anyone intercepting them."

"Really? It sounds like some ghastly ancient old hag of a woman from the Foreign Office," said Tom. And he realized how low Susan must be feeling by the fact that she actually laughed and didn't jump down his throat for making sexist jokes.

Miss Shepherd took her cookery classes in the actual kitchens of the school on the cook's day off. These rooms were the same as the original kitchens when Burlap Hall had been a private house, but the old iron stoves had been ripped out and replaced with huge catering ovens, and hanging from the walls were vast aluminium pots where once had hung neat rows of brass-bottomed saucepans. The great wooden tables used as chopping boards had been used for firewood and now long formica tables, criss-crossed with knife-marks, took their place; the old stone larder had been converted into one great humming freezer, packed with huge catering packs of frozen carrots, peas and beans.

Tom hated the kitchens because they always smelt of old fat and yesterday's cauliflower, all hung over with the decaying smell of washing-up water, probably trapped in the U-bends of the sinks that now filled up the great fireplace where once whole oxen roasted on spits.

"Today we will look at the bechamel or white sauce which is such an important base for so many other sauces — cheese sauce, parsley sauce, for instance — and is often used to thicken other dishes, like shepherd's pie or even stews," said Miss Shepherd. She'd managed to get up from her sick-bed to give the lesson but was still feeling rather woozy. She was so pale that the tip of her nose was now a normal colour. Tom hated parsley sauce, and he liked his shepherd's pie nice and ordinary like his mother made it, not all gunged up with a floury sauce.

That was another thing about school. The food! Had they never heard that it was healthier and more delicious to cook vegetables for *under* five hours rather than over? Didn't it occur to them that custard skin was disgusting? When they chose the meat at the butcher, didn't they know it was best to pick the bits that were mostly meat with the least fat on them rather than the other way around? And would it be too much to ask that they cooked real potatoes to mash, rather than provide a powdery dust they mixed with water? Still, at least Miss Shepherd's horrible idea gave him a chance to use the flour that Mr Fritz had given him. He cautiously pulled the packet towards him as Miss Shepherd demonstrated how to make the sauce.

"First, melt some margarine in your pans," she piped. She stood behind them as they all crowded round individual burners on the special stoves that had been set up for the school's cookery lessons. She ladled out several teaspoonfuls of margarine and everyone started stirring away as it slowly melted in each pan.

"When it has melted, add half a tablespoonful of flour until you have a stiff mixture that we call a roux. Now turn your gas down very low and start adding the milk, just a little at a time to prevent lumps forming."

Tom deliberately added a whole dollop of milk and when his sauce was nice and lumpy he called Miss Shepherd over.

"Miss, mine's got lumps," he said, pathetically. "Can you help me, please?"

"Mine hasn't," piped Rosemary from the next burner. "You added your milk too quickly."

Tom glared at her. "What did I tell you?" said Miss Shepherd petulantly. "Still it's probably a good example of what a white sauce should *not* look like." She came over to peer at the lumpy goo in Tom's saucepan. "There's only one way to solve that, and that is to stir and stir until all the lumps have gone. Give it to me." She took the spoon from Tom's hand and started to stir.

Susan and Miles were staring intently at her, wondering what her reaction would be. Would she scream and drop the spoon, as Mrs Grain had dropped the basket? Or would she faint?

Much to their disappointment nothing happened at all. Perhaps she hadn't been turned into a vampire. Perhaps she'd just had an ordinary cold when she'd been ill. They all felt disappointed. Then Tom wondered, could it be that there was so little flour in the mixture? Or that the blessing had been somehow cooked out of it? He suddenly had an idea and while she was busy stirring away he dipped his hand into the packet of flour and, behind her back, poured a small circle of flour on the floor around her feet.

She continued to stir and after a few minutes she

turned to Tom. "Now, look, it's much better, but there are still lumps and you'll never get them out unless you put the whole thing into a food processor, which is such an unpleasant, mechanical way of preparing food, wouldn't you agree?"

"Mine's very smooth," said Miles, who had spotted what Tom had done and wanted to to draw her away from the stove to his burner. ("It's *you* who's smooth," muttered Susan who hadn't noticed what had gone on. "Oily and smooth, just like this disgusting sauce.")

Miss Shepherd turned to come over to Miles, but something strange had happened. She was rooted to the spot. She made an attempt to move, but although her top half could sway freely, her feet stayed in the tiny circle of flour and she felt she would topple over. It was a horrible feeling, as if she were surrounded by some huge outside force, pressing her back. The more she tried to get out, the worse it got, until she felt overwhelmed by a feeling of pressure. She looked down and saw the flour and a vague realization came flooding over her. She drew back her lips in an evil snarl.

"Take this flour away!" she commanded, her voice sharp and cutting. As she spoke she wondered at herself. She was normally so peaceful and friendly to everyone. It didn't sound like her talking at all. *"If you don't take it away I will punish you!"* Her face was contorted with rage, her arms held high with horror and her fingers caught in a spasm, drawn sharply back from the palms.

The whole class had stopped stirring now, staring at Miss Shepherd in amazement. Sheila was about to push some of the flour away with her foot but Tom held her back. Miss Shepherd's face twisted and turned with fury, the tip of her nose getting redder and redder. "It's you, Tom Buxton," she hissed. "I will tell my Master of this. You have already created enough trouble! Be warned!" And with that she crouched down as far as she could and puffing with all her might she managed to blow part of the flour away. Then she staggered out of the circle.

It was funny, but now she was free of the flour circle she felt a lot better. She blinked a few times, then put her hand on Tom's shoulder, shaking her head. "Tom, I *am* sorry," she gushed, aimiably. "I don't know what came over me. It's not like me to lose my temper like that. I believe in peace and harmony among mankind and I apologize. I'm afraid it must be this illness. I do feel very queer."

But as she spoke she heard a distant voice, speaking to her from far away.

"Do not apologize," it said. It was a dark, foggy, booming voice, which seemed to speak from the mists of time. "You have done well. I am your Master. You will do everything I ask. You will become as I am, one of the great undead. Soon the undead will rule the world. You are my servant. You will obey me in all things." Suddenly Miss Shepherd felt extremely faint and peculiar.

"If you'll forgive me, we'll end the lesson there," she said in a feeble voice. "I think I must go and lie down."

Everyone in the class was jabbering with surprise after the incident but Tom, Miles and Susan didn't wait to talk and washed up their pans quicker than they'd ever done before. They were determined to find Mr Fritz and tell him what had happened, but as they rushed out of the door they bumped into Asquith Minor in the hall who'd just returned from a run with Mr Carstairs. Lots of the other pupils were clustered round him as he talked.

"You should have seen Carstairs' face!" he said, clutching his sides. "He'd been moaning at me all the time for not taking running seriously – who would, jolly boring if you ask me – and insisted I keep up with him. Well, you know me, never take a train if you can fly, never drive if you can take a train, never run if you can drive..."

"Oh, get on with it," shouted someone in the group around him.

"Well, there I was puffing along with the old lungs pumping away, practically dead through lack of oxygen when we got to the stream. By this time I was nearly in my grave, but being a good old trooper, I leapt over the stream like a fawn and was limping along through the woods when I suddenly realized old Carstairs wasn't with me. Had he sped ahead of me, like an antelope, I wondered? Had he taken off and started to fly? I stopped to get my breath and tottered to the end of the woods but he was nowhere to be seen. Could it be that he had actually fallen behind? Was it a case of the tortoise and the hare being re-enacted in the grounds of Burlap Hall, with AM playing tortoise and Carstairs playing hare?"

"Oh, get a move on," yelled someone else. "Your mind's wandering!"

"Yeah, watch out, it's too small to wander," yelled another boy. "It might get lost!"

"May I continue?" said Asquith Minor, irritably.

"As I was saying. I wondered if the old greased lightning hadn't had an accident. So, thinking I'd do my good deed for the day, remembering the days when I was a Cub – not so long ago, actually – I loped back through the old undergrowth to see if he'd twisted an ankle. But not a bit of it. When I got back to the river, there was old Carstairs on the other side looking *completely mad*, battling away to try to cross the stream. Every time he tried, he fell back as if he were being pushed by an invisible hand. I tried to help him across but it was impossible. Eventually I said: 'Don't worry, sir, you're probably a bit tired, it must be your age.'"

"You *didn't*!" said someone, incredulously.

"I jolly well did," said Asquith Minor, nodding his head vigorously. "And the poor old chap, looking rather more like a dusty five watt bulb than greased lightning, I'll tell you, had to turn around and stagger back to school the other way. Pathetic!"

Miles, Susan and Tom all looked at each other. Miles nodded. "Running water," he whispered. "Vampires hate running water. So Carstairs has been got at, too. That leaves only Mr Fritz and old Fox."

They didn't have a chance to talk to Mr Fritz because he was teaching. Then it was more lessons for them and tea. They'd have to nobble him later. But just before their meal the post was distributed. There was a letter for Tom, at last. It was from his parents. He tore it open. Thank goodness. Perhaps they'd come and take him away. Surely, they'd at least have made enquiries, or done *something*. But this is what it said:

Dear Tom,

I am afraid we have some very bad news for you. Your grandmother died two days ago. We are all so sad and hope you won't be too upset – even though you knew it was coming. I would have replied to your letter earlier – but I have to say we were very upset to get it, especially as your new biology teacher, Mr Culard, had been so kind as to deliver it by hand as he was in London at the time. It was a particularly bad moment for you to play such a joke on us, I'm afraid. It was lucky we had asked Mr Culard in for a cup of tea because he was able to reassure us that there has been a spate of this silliness at your school and he convinced us not to take it seriously. Vampires indeed!

As I was so busy, Mr Culard had a very long chat with Dad till quite late and said he would be dealing with you firmly. I hope it's not too firmly because that letter was so out of the ordinary for you. It all sounds most odd, but Mr Culard was so kind and even said he'd look in on us again one night when he was next in town – it seems he travels down quite often.

Please, Tom, don't do this sort of thing again. It is really childish behaviour.

Sadly, we won't be able to have you back for half-term, by the way, because it's Granny's funeral then and we both have to go up north today to sort out all the arrangements with the solicitors and undertakers and so on, so you'll have to stay at school. I'm sure there'll be some other of your friends staying too, so you won't be too lonely. We've written to Mr Fox to explain things.

Must rush. Just after Mr Culard left, Dad went down with an awful bug and I've been feeding him up with juicy steaks as they're the only thing he seems to want these days. I think he got ill because he was so upset about Granny. I must say he's very edgy and irritable — when I gave him a steak with garlic sauce on it yesterday he threw it at the wall in a fit of temper! So unlike him. Still I must be patient with him because he's very unhappy and people often behave rather erratically when they're unhappy.

Longing to see you at the end of term.

Lots and lots of love,

Mum

CHAPTER SEVEN

Try as they might to report back to Mr Fritz about the latest developments, it seemed impossible. He was either teaching or out somewhere. When they got up to his room eventually that day, a note on his study door announced: "Back in one hour". But as he'd failed to say what time he'd put it up, it wasn't much help to Miles, Tom and Susan as they turned gloomily from his door and walked despairingly down the corridor.

"He's probably discussing with Mr Culard how to get rid of us," said Miles. "That stuff about the flour was probably a trap he set us to see how much we knew."

"Nonsense," said Susan. "I've been thinking. I think Mr Fritz is OK. I bet he wears garlic down his vest to protect himself. Even I've found myself wearing a crucifix my mother gave me..." and she fished down her shirt front and hauled up a tiny silver cross on a silver chain.

"What else have you got down there?" asked Miles, getting up on tiptoe and staring down her front.

"Never you mind!" said Susan, putting her hand up to her throat.

"Don't worry, you've always got me to protect you," said Miles, putting his arm round her in a joky way.

"You! I need someone to protect me from you, I don't need you to protect me!" replied Susan, wriggling out from under his arm, laughing.

Miles started pretending to cry. "Now you've hurt my feelings," he said in a baby voice.

"Oh, poor little Milesy-wilesy," said Susan, coming

up to him. "Who's a diddums then?"

While they were fooling around Tom felt lonelier and lonelier. He lagged behind on his own, wishing someone understood how he felt. After his mother's letter he was sick with worry about what had happened at home. Could Mr Culard really have attacked his dad? It was too horrible to think about. And would his mother be safe? If only he could go home at half-term he might be able to do something. As it was he'd be stuck at Burlap Hall while everyone else was away – except perhaps Sheila, who was no help. And, of course, Mr Culard. Maybe he should just run away and go back home anyway? But how would he get into his house? His parents wouldn't be there, they'd be away at the funeral. And he never brought his front door key to school.

Down the other end of the corridor Susan and Miles were still mucking around as if they'd forgotten about Tom's existence. He dragged his feet along the floor slowly; he felt so gloomy he could hardly put one step in front of the other. He didn't really want to reach the others, anyway. When Susan and Miles were giggling together like this, he always felt left out.

"Aren't you coming?" called Susan, turning round to him.

"You go on ahead," said Tom. But his voice came out all croaky and Susan wandered back up to him. When she saw his long face she looked concerned.

"Hey, cheer up," she said kindly. "What's the matter? We'll see Mr Fritz soon. He's only gone out for a while."

Tom couldn't speak. He just stared at the floor and shook his head.

"Did you hear from your parents?" asked Susan, in a

low voice so Miles wouldn't hear.

Tom stopped and wearily pulled out his mother's letter from his pocket. Susan read it through; as she did so, her face changed.

"This is terrible," she breathed. "Terrible, terrible. Mr Culard's been to see your parents!"

Miles wandered up and Susan whirled round to show him the letter. "Look at this! Tom wrote to his parents telling them about the school being full of vampires –" Tom was grateful she didn't mention about him asking to be taken home – "and look what's happened!"

Miles read the letter and his expression turned to one of horror.

"If I could go home for half-term I could explain to Mum what might have happened to Dad, but I can't because my grandmother's died and they're going away. At least Mum seems safe for the moment," said Tom. "But for how long?"

"Well, *I'm* going to be here at half-term anyway, because I *never* go home at half-term because my Mom and Pop are abroad. There are a couple of other kids here at half-term, too, so we won't be completely alone. Now come on, Miles, how about you staying on, too? It's no good you giving out all this talk of being here to protect me if you aren't, is it? And we've got to stick together in a situation like this."

"Oh, come on, you can't ask Miles to give up his half-term just because of us," said Tom, though he felt very grateful to Susan for suggesting it.

"I suppose I could always ring my parents from the phone-box in the village and say I wanted to stay on because we were rehearsing a special play or some-thing," said Miles, doubtfully, "but how would I clear it with Mr Fox?"

"Oh, you just assume he knows. He's so hopeless. If you say your parents wrote him a letter saying you must stay on, he won't argue. He'll just think he lost it. OK – so will you stay?"

"We–ell...all right," said Miles. "I wouldn't really feel happy going home and leaving you two here, I must say."

Later that night, when Miles had returned from the village after making his call, Tom felt he had to say something.

"It's really nice of you, Miles, to give up your half-term you know," he said, rather embarrassedly as he stood by the basin in his pyjamas, squeezing toothpaste onto his brush.

"Oh, rubbish," said Miles, as he took off his shirt. "Though it was a bit difficult explaining it to them because they'd just got this letter I'd written to them, asking to come home earlier than usual. I didn't like to mention it before because I thought Susan would think I was being pathetic."

Tom grinned at himself in the mirror through a moustache of bubbled toothpaste.

"Gyate minds hink ayike," he said; then he rinsed his mouth out and spat into the basin. "I mean 'great minds think alike,'" he repeated. "I did just the same. Come on," he added, leaping into bed. "What's on telly tonight?"

For most of this term, Mr Fox had been feeling as if he were on the edge of a nervous breakdown. Every day one or other of his staff was ill with this mysterious bug that was going around. The only consolation so far was that none of the children seemed to have caught it.

And the teachers appeared to get over it quite quickly — but they weren't quite the same as before when they recovered. It was no good Mr Fox ticking off the pupils for looking scruffy when all the teachers were going around looking like a bunch of tramps. Some had even stopped having baths and were, quite frankly, starting to smell. He'd had to sit next to Mrs Grain at tea and he could hardly put up with the whiff. He'd been shocked and astonished, too, to see Miss Shepherd in the corridor, the day before, tucking into a bag of fresh mince. She'd looked terrible, stuffing it into her mouth like an animal, with long strings of it hanging down her chin.

Traditionally, the day before half-term was the day of the annual school photograph. Mr Fox had learnt through long experience that both pupils and staff always looked a lot jollier when they knew they were going home the next day and for the last few years the school photos had shown happy, smiling teachers and children, as if they were auditioning for a West End run of *Oklahoma!* — a nice change from the days when they looked like inmates of Alcatraz. But even so, however cheerful a sight they were, he couldn't allow the teachers to appear unkempt in a photograph that parents would see, so he summoned his staff to an evening meeting.

As they all shuffled into the Staff Room Mr Fox was frankly appalled. Even Mr Culard, who had been coerced into making an appearance for the photograph, looked quite smart and dapper compared to the bedraggled bunch of staff. Mr Fox had had to be very firm with him. He couldn't send parents a school photo with no biology teacher present. As it turned out, Mr Culard's looks had improved. He seemed to have filled out a bit, as if he'd had a few good meals since arriving at Burlap Hall. And Mr Fritz, who usually looked like a man who had swum in his clothes over Niagara Falls and then dried himself off in the wind, looked positively suave and elegant in comparison with the rest.

Mr Fox stood up and tapped on a table to get their attention.

There was still some muttering in a corner and Mr Fox could hear Mr Roy and Signor Ruzzi discussing steaks and how they both preferred them rare, almost raw. He tapped louder, cleared his throat and started working his ears and eyebrows around for one of his famous "looks". This had the desired effect and soon there was complete silence.

"I find it sad that the day has come," intoned Mr Fox, keeping the look going even though he was talking, "when I have to assemble my staff and reprimand them for their sloppy appearance. I have been so proud of you in the past, a well-turned out bunch, who usually look so smart and well-groomed — a credit to Burlap Hall. But in recent weeks your high standards have been deteriorating sadly. I would describe your appearance as pessimissimus in the extreme." Mrs Grain started to object but Mr Fox held up his hand firmly. "I said pessimissimus and I meant pessimissimus," he said, glaring. "And because tomorrow morning we have the school photograph, I would like you to make a particular effort to spruce up a bit. How long is it, for instance, since any of you have had a bath?"

There was a little scream of horror from Miss Shepherd. "Not a bath!" she whispered. "Not running water!"

The other teachers seemed to agree. "Running water is disgusting," exclaimed Mrs Grain. "I hate the horrible way it burbles out of the tap. Ugh!"

"I don't care whether you have a bath or a shower or even a sponge-down," said Mr Fox, "but you must at least be clean. And it seems to me that some of you, whose names shall be nameless –" he gave an embarrassed cough to cover his error – "have forgotten how to use a comb or a hairbrush!"

"It's not the combs," snorted Mr Carstairs. "The combs are fine. But there's something very weird about my mirror!"

Mr Roy agreed. "I can hardly see myself in mine," he complained. "I don't know if it's my eyes or what. I can see everything else quite clearly."

"Well, find a mirror that works!" snapped Mr Fox. "I don't care what you do, but you must all smarten up considerably for tomorrow's picture! At the moment you all look like a bunch of hippies off to celebrate the solstice at Stonehenge!"

There was a general muttering as the teachers talked between themselves, complaining how unfair Mr Fox was being. Mr Fox didn't mind. He had a duty to do. What *did* upset him, however, was the presence of Mr Culard, who stood at the back, staring at him intently, a grim, ghastly smile fixed on his pale face.

It was not a good day for a photograph. Grey storm-clouds bulging with warm rain loomed overhead. There was a cold, wild wind blowing, tossing the branches of the trees till they danced in an overture to what surely was going be a gigantic storm. As he walked over the front lawn with the other pupils to take his place in the picture, Tom felt the air jumping with electricity and danger; had he been an animal he was certain all his fur would have been fluffed up and his ears pricked in anticipation of a mighty downpour.

Mr Fox was stage-managing the event with the aid of a loud-hailer. "CLASS WUNN-CEE," he yelled, "OVER ON THE RIGHT! CLASS TWO-DEE — MOVE YOUR BOTTOMS TO MAKE ROOM!" And so on, until the whole school was finally assembled on the lawn in straight rows, facing a frantic photographer from Lanchester.

"I'm just going to take a couple of Polaroids as testers!" he yelled. "So everyone, look happy! It's half-term tomorrow!"

Everyone duly pulled horrible faces and stuck their tongues out until Mr Fox's ears began to move as if a look was coming and they started to behave themselves.

The photographer seemed pleased enough with the Polaroids and chucked them on the grass before he gave a thumbs-up sign to Mr Fox, who seated himself in the centre of the huge group. All the girls looked as charming as possible — with the exception of Susan, who glowered, and Rosemary, who tried to look like a dying swan. Then the photographer started snapping away for the official picture, taken, as always, in two sections. Asquith Minor was caught running round from one half to another to appear twice and was forced to sit cross-legged by Mr Fox's feet until finally huge splats of rain started lurching from the sky, as if someone had punctured the clouds with a skewer. At last the photographer, with an eye to his equipment, signalled that he had finished. The entire school hared across the lawn, the girls screaming, the younger boys pulling their blazers over their heads and the older boys sauntering casually, trying to pretend they didn't care a pin about getting soaked to the skin. But eventually everyone was back in Burlap Hall and the bell started ringing for lunch.

"Where's Susan?" Miles asked Tom as they waited in line for a huge dollop of overcooked spaghetti to be whacked onto their waiting plates.

"Isn't she sitting with us?"

"I dunno," said Tom, helping himself to ketchup to boost the measly portion of sauce that had come his way. "Maybe she got caught in the rain."

He felt wet and miserable. The letter from his mother had really upset him. It wasn't so much about his granny, it was the fact that she hadn't trusted him and had listened to Mr Culard instead. She'd thought he'd played some ridiculous trick on them – the last thing he'd ever do. Of course, to be fair on her, Mr Culard no doubt was at his most persuasive. But what had he done to his dad? And would there be any way of helping him? In a way Tom felt it was lucky that it had started raining and they were all soaked because when the odd drip fell from his face onto the spaghetti, Miles would think it was a drop of rain. In fact it was tears – and he was crying because he felt so alone and frightened. And powerless. Even the episode with the flour didn't really prove anything, whatever Mr Fritz said. It would only be Miss Shepherd's word against theirs. And could they even trust Mr Fritz?

They'd finished the spaghetti by the time Susan squelched in, her hair trickling down her face in sodden strings and her clothes, transparent with the rain, sticking wetly to her body.

She wriggled in between Tom and Miles who shifted away from her to avoid getting wet. "You're soaking!" exclaimed Miles, pointing to the floor beneath her where a pool of water was already forming. "Go and get dry! We'll all be wet soon. You know what they say about osmosis." But Susan ignored him.

"I've got the most *incredible* thing!" she hissed, pulling a small square of paper from under her dripping coat. "I stayed behind to pick up the Polaroids! Just look at these!"

Tom and Miles both moved closer and craned over her shoulders to see what she was on about.

"Can you see Mr Culard?" whispered Susan. "No, you can't. Because he really *is* a vampire. Vampires can't see themselves in mirrors because mirrors are meant to reflect the soul. And that's why some Arabs don't like you taking photographs of them because they think it steals their souls. But Mr Culard's got no soul to steal because he's undead and that's why he doesn't come out in the photograph!

"And look at Mr Roy, Mrs Grain, Miss Shepherd and Signor Ruzzi. See how faint they are! This is absolute proof that what we say is true. We must see Mr Fritz and tell him. We've got to stop talking about all this and start *doing* something!"

Tom couldn't help feeling a twinge of admiration for her. And he felt cheered by this new piece of evidence. He even offered to get her some spaghetti, but as he spoke, Miles had already scrambled to his feet to go and get her some himself.

Mr Fritz had had a quick lunch and gone up to his study to dry off. His wood fire was blazing and as he stood in front of it, warming himself, faint plumes of steam rose from his hairy suit, mingling with the smoke from his pipe. He felt damp and anxious. Even though he was almost certain that Mr Culard *was* a vampire, he still couldn't really be sure. One minute he was positive, the next he held back from taking any further steps. After all, schools were notorious as places where hysteria could take hold; there were stories of entire classes suffering from faintness and sickness all at the same time, a hysterical reaction to just one member falling ill. And he had to remind himself that at the beginning of term he'd only just come back from holidaying in a village that was rife with vampire-talk; perhaps he'd communicated his own fears and fantasies to the children when he talked to them about it on the first day of term? After all, children were full of fanciful ideas. Probably Tom and Miles had *thought* they saw Mr Culard walking down the wall but in fact it was just the effect of over-heated imaginations. Not that either of those two had ever seemed anything but sensible; but he knew that school, particularly boarding school, could wreak strange changes on children and masters alike.

It was when he was in the middle of this reverie that there was a knock on the door and Miles, Tom and Susan burst in to tell him the latest news. They'd decided that it was better to risk confiding everything in Mr Fritz than saying nothing. None of them knew a thing about vampires and, as Miles pointed out, if they did nothing they would end up being bitten by Mr Culard, and if Mr Fritz were a vampire the only thing he could do was bite them – which would happen to them anyway. But if he wasn't a vampire – then there was a chance of defeating Mr Culard.

The first encouraging thing that they noticed when they entered Mr Fritz's study was the fact that there were curious strings of what looked like onions hanging around the doors and window-frames.

"It's garlic!" whispered Tom to Miles. "He can't be a vampire if he's protecting himself from them!"

"Indeed I am not!" said Mr Fritz, who had overheard them. "You poor children! Did you think I might be in league with Mr Culard? Why, of course you did!" he added, seeing their blushing faces. "It seems as if none of us has been completely frank with the other, eh? I thought you might be imagining things – and you thought I might be a vampire. Indeed not. Look!" And he picked a piece of garlic from one of the garlands and popped it into his mouth. "It'll make my breath smell, but at least it'll prove to you that I am Mr Culard's greatest enemy!"

After he'd heard about Miss Shepherd and the flour, read the letter from Tom's mother and seen the Polaroids, he became most decisive.

"We must act," he said, emphatically, puffing furiously on his pipe.

"But how?" asked Tom, Miles and Susan. They sat on the floor looking up at him trustingly.

"Anyway," added Tom, "what exactly *is* a vampire? Why do they exist? What do they want?"

Mr Fritz leant back and closed his eyes.

"Vampires," he said in a hushed voice, "are wicked people whose souls are so evil that they can never rest. In Romania it is thought that suicides turned into vampires and as a result they were always buried at crossroads, the idea being that when, at night, they woke to haunt their fellow men, they would spend most of the night pondering which route to take, and dawn would come before they could set off to perform their evil tasks.

"Vampires are the undead, people of the night, and they can live, if you can call it living, for hundreds and hundreds of years. But in order to exist, they need fresh blood to feed on. So at night, they roam the countryside, sometimes changing into animal shape, looking for supplies.

"After a vampire has fed enough upon a person, he will then force that person to drink *his* blood and thus turn him into a vampire himself. That's what's happening to the other teachers at the moment. They are aware they don't feel well. Mr Culard may have already talked to some of them in their dreams. But they're not sure what's going on. They're not fully-formed vampires yet. And nor, Tom, is your father, who you must be worrying about. Although Mr Culard has begun his evil work, all the people he's attacked so far are still able to go about their daily business up to a point – though soon, of course, Mr Culard will initiate them into full-blooded, if you'll excuse the expression, vampires, by getting them to drink his blood.

"Until this final ceremony, in which he comes to them at night, opens a vein in his own chest and forces them to drink from the gushing fountain of blood that springs out, they have a chance of turning back into completely normal human beings. But once he has performed this ceremony, they will be vampires for ever after unless they are destroyed by special means which I'll go into later. My own feeling is that he is preparing the ground at this stage. Then he will take a bride – for he needs a bride to help in his evil work. And then they will both take on the great task of initiating all the teachers — and after that, of course, they'll start on the children.

"I have looked into the whole matter very thoroughly and indeed have read an excellent book on the subject by the world-famous vampire expert, Montague Summers. Would you like me to read you what he says of vampires?"

Tom, Miles and Susan all nodded silently, while Mr Fritz got up from his deep armchair and fumbled about with some papers on a table nearby. Eventually he found the book, an old, gnarled, leather-covered volume with slips of paper protruding where he'd marked certain passages. He sat down with it on his knee, opened it, and started to read.

"'A vampire is generally described as being exceedingly gaunt and lean with a hideous countenance and eyes wherein are glinting the red fire of perdition,'" he began.

"That's Mr Culard!" said Tom. "His eyes are just like that!"

"Wait. Let me read on. Please don't interrupt," said Mr Fritz. "'When, however, he has satiated his lust for warm human blood, his body becomes horribly puffed and bloated, as though he were some great leech, gorged and replete to bursting. Cold as ice, or it may be fevered and burning as a hot coal, the skin is deathly pale, but the lips are very full and rich, blub and red; the teeth white and gleaming, and the canine teeth wherewith he bites deep into the neck of his prey to suck thence the vital streams which reanimate his body and invigorate all his forces appear notably sharp and pointed. Often his mouth curls back in a vulpine snarl which bares these fangs. It is said that the palms of a vampire's hands are downy with hair, and the nails are always curved and crooked, often well-nigh the length of a great bird's claw, the quicks dirty and foul with clots and gouts of black blood. His breath is unbearably fetid and rank with corruption, the stench of the charnel' — that's a slaughterhouse."

"Yes, have you seen his nails?" cried Susan. "They're really horrible!"

"And his breath — ugh!" added Miles.

"But how can we stop him?" asked Tom. "We surely can't kill him. I know you're meant to drive a stake through their hearts — I suppose to stop them wandering about — but none of us could do that, even to Mr Culard. And say we'd made a mistake? We'd all be sent for youth custody — or at best, detention centres for short, sharp shocks! Or worse still, long, sharp shocks! And afterwards we'd never be able to get jobs!" As he said this he was guiltily reminded of how like his father he sounded.

"Speaking personally, I think I'm a bit old for youth custody," said Mr Fritz, smiling slightly. "I'd be in for life at Wormwood Scrubs or some such institution. And I doubt if I'd be able to continue my teaching career even if I ever lived to experience freedom again.

"There are other ways of killing vampires, too. One way to destroy Mr Culard would be to burn him by fire. Or we could drown him in a stream of running water. And there are yet other methods, though I forget exactly what they are. Vampires can, of course, be halted in their activities because they certainly hate the sign of the cross, garlic and broad sunlight, which is why Mr Culard will only teach in the afternoons, when the sun is going down."

"What does he do at night?" asked Susan. "Apart from change into a bat and fly into people's rooms to bite them, that is? Doesn't he need any rest?"

"Indeed he does, and every vampire has to sleep in a coffin" — Miles gave a gasp — "filled with soil from his native land. Somewhere, Mr Culard must have a coffin, probably at his lodgings, in which he sleeps. It might be an idea, during half-term, to discover this coffin when he is up and about, and try to dispose of it so that at least he'll have no resting-place. It might be worth filling his mouth with garlic while he sleeps, or draping his sleeping quarters with wild rose or whitethorn — which vampires hate."

"Or we could say the Lord's Prayer over him," suggested Susan. "That'd give him nightmares."

"Daymares," corrected Tom. "He's up and about during the night, remember."

"I'm sure that would hamper him but I doubt it would keep him trapped for long," said Mr Fritz. "Remember his powers are getting stronger and stronger the more blood he drinks. That's why he was able to take part in the school photo even though it was daylight. Not that it did him much good, of course."

"I wonder why he agreed to take part," mused Miles. "Why didn't he just stay at home?"

"Mr Fox is very pernickety about things like that. And no doubt Mr Culard realized that it would be several weeks before the official film was developed. By which time he would have taken over the whole school." Mr Fritz gave a slight shudder as he spoke.

"Won't putting garlic in his coffin just make him madder than ever?" asked Susan. "What we want is to get rid of him for good."

"What we must do," said Mr Fritz, putting the tips of his fingers together, "is to delay his activities until we have found a foolproof way to destroy him, a method that will put none of us at risk. Even if we were to kill Mr Culard, after all, by one of the methods I've described, it's quite possible we would be accused of murder and no judge would believe that he was a vampire. In Romania, we might get away with it. But not in the county of Lanchestershire, England.

"No, what I must do is return to Romania this half-term and consult my friends there. I will return with a method that we will be able to use without risk. I have an idea of what it is, but we can't put it into practice unless we get all details absolutely correct. We can't afford to fail. Then we would be done for. In the meantime I will leave you to discover Mr Culard's dwelling place. And any other relevant information." He paused, looking worriedly at their upturned faces. They looked so young and innocent. It was wicked that Mr Culard should inflict such anxiety on children.

"Protect yourselves, all of you, won't you?" he said, in a low and urgent voice. "I don't want to come back and find any of you undead. I'd never forgive myself."

"I've got my crucifix," said Susan.

"Miles and I could use some garlic," Tom said, pulling two bulbs from Mr Fritz's garland. "We'll string one each round our necks to keep us safe."

"Excellent," said Mr Fritz, leaning forward and rubbing his hands over the fire. "And as for Mr Culard..." he added, staring deep into the glowing coals, "his days are numbered."

CHAPTER EIGHT

During half-term the school had an eerie feel to it, like a ghost town. The cloakrooms featured rows of empty hooks, with just the occasional forgotten bag hanging in solitary splendour, like a scene from the *Marie Celeste*. Tom, Miles and Susan and a couple of juniors with washed-out faces had their meals alone in the school dining room, their voices bouncing off the walls of the empty hall and booming uncharacteristically. The one cook left to cater for them did the minimum of work; all their meals were salads. Mr Fox didn't eat with them, thank heavens, preferring to take his meals alone in his study, with a little liquid refreshment from the bottles behind the copies of Lowe's *Latin Primer*. All the other teachers had returned to their various homes except Mr Carstairs who stayed in his room alone most of the time, popping out only occasionally for the odd run in the evening. He didn't even eat with them. Tom noticed that since the Asquith Minor affair he had changed his route; now he simply ran several times round the lawn to avoid the stream.

Life at half-term was dead boring. They were allowed to watch the staff television set for a couple of hours daily – an experience that Miles and Tom found rather overwhelming since they'd got so used to seeing entire programmes peopled by characters a quarter of an inch high. Now and again Mr Fox initiated a ponderous game of Scrabble in his study, always winning by using words like Zogoax, Juxtant and Quoggip which he assured them were old Anglo-Saxon, though they could never find them in the dictionary. They were allowed to use the only computer game in the school – chess – in which the computer always won; they had free access to the library at all times of the day or night – with the chance of dipping into such thrilling works as *The European Community: How It Works, The History of the Telephone* and *Mysticism and Reality: Is There a Choice?*

But there was really nothing interesting to do at all, particularly as none of them felt they could relax – partly because of the presence of Mr Fox but mainly because of the fear of being attacked by Mr Culard. Since no one was keeping much of an eye on them, Susan sneaked into their room at night and took it in turns to sleep in each of their beds while one of them slept on the floor.

"Talk about equality," moaned Miles one night as he bedded down by the door. "Why can't *you* sleep on the floor for once?"

"I have my reasons," Susan replied mysteriously, and the matter was dropped until Miles persisted and she explained: "I am your guest. Were you my guests in *my* room, *I* would naturally sleep on the floor."

Tom didn't think much of this and Miles' discomfort on the floor certainly overcame any excitement he might have felt about Susan sleeping in their room.

Each night they would take it in turns to keep watch. Tom would stay awake the first hour, then wake Miles who would keep awake for another hour before waking Susan. Luckily it didn't matter how late they slept in. They had said the Lord's Prayer over a basin of water and made the sign of the cross with the water over the keyhole and the cracks in the doors and windows, and they also kept the lights blazing until Mr

Fox noticed the gleaming window and came and yelled at them to turn them off.

To find out where Mr Culard lived – if lived was the word – was easier said than done. For the first two days they thought he had gone away for half-term as well as the rest of the teachers – until Susan pointed out that it would be too difficult for him to go away for longer than a night, since presumably he had to be back in his coffin, or wherever he resided, by dawn every morning. Then one evening when Miles had gone down to the village to get some sweets, he'd caught sight of Mr Culard lurking near the graveyard. Apparently he had smiled a ghastly smile at him and said: "Ah, young Miles! Here for half-term, then? I will perhaps come and visit you one night and we will discuss the mysteries of life and death together, yes?" Miles had stammered some reply and hurtled back to Burlap Hall with the news.

Finally they agreed to get up in the very early morning, long before dawn and, liberally equipped with garlic and holy flour, hang about the grounds to see if they could see any signs of him – then follow him back to his lair.

"But what if Mr Fox sees us?" asked Miles. "Even at half-term he'd surely not allow us to go roaming about just before dawn? It'll be pitch black."

"He won't know, stupid," says Susan. "He never gets up before eleven, haven't you noticed?"

"We'll say we're going to pick mushrooms," said Tom, brightly.

"Mushrooms? You must be joking! I bet they don't grow at this time of year!" said Susan.

"Well, Mr Fox doesn't know what time of the year mushrooms grow, either," said Tom defensively.

So at 4.30 a.m. the following morning, after they'd all been woken by a chorus of squeaking from their digital watches, the three of them struggled out of bed, dragged on their clothes, tiptoed down the stairs and sneaked out of the front door feeling like criminals. And also feeling like death, since it was far too early for any normal human being to be up and about.

"Where do we go? I can't see a thing," whispered Susan, clutching Tom's arm as they crept down the drive in the darkness. And it was only because of the crunch of gravel under their feet that they knew it was the drive at all. The night huddled round them like damp velvet; just to walk through the darkness was like pushing through black custard. It was so dark they could hardly tell if their eyes were open or not because it made no difference either way; and because they could see nothing, they felt they were going to bump into something any minute – for all they knew they might have been surrounded by walls waiting to be crashed into, or precipices waiting to be fallen over. The chill in the air seemed to have frozen out any kind of smell; there was no sound at all except the odd leaf giving up the ghost and dropping to the ground.

Very gradually their eyes started to accustom themselves to the darkness. They could make out the trunks of trees, the outline of the hall itself, black against an even blacker sky. The vast lawn looked like a huge pool of water; then slowly familiar bumps could be made out, greyly silver in the light of a fading moon.

"Look!" Miles pointed upwards. "Isn't that Mr Carstairs' room?"

There was a faint glimmering coming from the window, as if a glow-worm danced within. As they stared, they heard the familar squeaking of a bat which chirrupped and chattered in the night air.

"Where is it?" whispered Miles, scanning the sky. "We must follow it! It must be Mr Culard!"

The squeaking faded away, leaving them baffled and dispirited – but just as they had nearly given up hope, the bat swooped past them, darting and diving, fluttering in mid-air, then shooting off in a different direction.

"Over there!" hissed Tom, who had caught a glimpse of its spiky, black outline against the moon. The others stumbled after him but soon lost him in the night and Tom pursued the creature alone, crashing through the woods, losing the bat and then waiting, breath held tight, until he heard its high-pitched chatter and he could creep along after it as quickly as he could.

There was a moment when he called out to Miles and was struck by a dart of fear when he realized that he was alone. For a second he considered going back, but it was too dark to know which way to turn. Then the bat suddenly swooped down nearby and he felt he couldn't abandon the chase when he had got so far.

He seemed to have been following it for a good quarter of an hour, over fields, through undergrowth, past copses and streams, over a main road and deep into another wood, when suddenly the sound stopped. Tom waited for about ten minutes but there was no sign of its by now familiar chirrup. Damn it. He must have lost it. He was about to turn back when he realized he had absolutely no idea where he was. Then it occurred to him: perhaps this was where the bat – or, rather, Mr Culard – actually lived. Perhaps he was near his lair.

He looked around in the blackness. Although his eyes had somewhat accustomed themselves to the dark, he still could hardly see a thing. But he soon realized that he was in the middle of a wood. Vast, knobbly tree trunks loomed at him from nowhere and great spidery branches groped down at him as he stepped carefully about, trying to find his bearings. Occasionally a night creature, surprised by the sound of his footsteps, would scuttle away into the leaves making a terrifying rustling sound. He was so frightened he could practically hear his heart beating; he could certainly feel it bumping against his shirt like a bouncing ball trying to get free. A slow trickle of warm slime ran down his cheek and he stopped in terror, imagining a horrible beast in the branches above, dribbling down on him. It took him a few petrified minutes to realize that it was simply a trickle of his own sweat.

He sat down by a tree trunk, determined to sit it out till it got light enough to know where he was, but he couldn't relax. His whole body was tense, his fists clenched by his side and even his toes seemed to be scrunched in panic inside his shoes. What was that? Every bone in his body froze as he heard a faint howling sound, like the cries of a starving child. He pressed his head back onto the bark and felt his eyes bulging out of his head. The sound got louder and louder, a high wailing sound – and then he remembered Signor Ruzzi's recent piano lessons. What was it he'd said? "And now – the howling of the wolves – ah, the children of the night – what music they make!" Nearer and nearer the sound came and soon Tom could hear the soft shuffling of an animal. There was the horrible, rank smell of old zoos, and to his horror he realized the wolf – if that was what it was – must be close by. Staring so hard he felt his eyes might soon pop from his head, he made out two glowing red eyes, apparently staring at him in the dark. Then, with a brief blood-curdling howl which split through the night air, the vision disappeared and Tom was left on his own.

He sat there for what seemed like hours, waiting for the dawn. Finally it was light enough to see a little.

He looked at his watch. It was 7.40. He just wished he had something to eat. He was absolutely starving. He was also freezing cold. He crept along a mossy bank and found a damp hole of leaves where he sat down for a few minutes, hoping that the dawn would thaw out his fear along with his limbs and enable him to recover. Every bone ached as the panic of the night's experience slowly drained from him and eventually he fell asleep.

When he woke an hour later the birds were singing and the autumn sun was out, filtering palely through the web of bare branches above him. Tom shivered. Thank goodness it was light at last. Far away he heard the low drone of a car. He must be somewhere near the road, he thought, so taking good note of his position and leaving a trail of carefully-arranged stones behind him, he slowly walked in the direction of the sound and eventually landed up at the crossroads in the centre of Burlap village opposite the post office. The Olde Tea Shoppe was just opening for morning coffee and he rummaged in his pocket for some money. He had enough for a cup of coffee and a bun so he treated himself to a breakfast that tasted as ancient as the old crone who served him, before going back to Burlap Hall to tell the others what had happened. He only hoped they were OK.

"What happened to you? We've been worried sick about you!" Miles looked drawn with worry when

Tom at last got back to the school. Susan had kindly gone down to the kitchens to rustle up some breakfast for him. As there were no staff around there wasn't a risk of being caught.

"We couldn't sleep for worry," said Miles. "We thought Mr Culard had got you."

"No. I'm fine. But what happened to you?" Tom couldn't help feeling flattered that both of them had clearly been so distressed by his absence.

"We started off after you but then you just disappeared. We called and called for you but there was no answer so we came back here. When it got light we started to look for you but we still couldn't find you. Thank goodness you're safe."

"It's horribly frightening all this, isn't it?" said Tom, casually. Since he'd been so brave in rushing after the bat on his own, he felt he could afford to show a little weakness, even to Miles.

"I'll say!" said Miles. "I don't mind telling you that if it hadn't been for Susan being around yesterday I had half a mind simply to run away and go home. If we get through all this and out the other side, I think we ought to be awarded a special bravery medal."

"Who'd nominate us?" said Tom, smiling. "Everyone would think it was invented. And who knows if we will get through it all, anyway?"

"Exactly, that's what I'm worried ab— Of course we will!" said Miles, changing the tone of his voice as Susan came into the dining room with a mug of tea and three slices of buttered toast. "No question about it!"

When Tom told them of his discovery they were keen to go off straight away and search the woods but Tom insisted on having a quick shower before they left. He felt covered with dead leaves and mould. So it was midday by the time they got down to the crossroads to retrace Tom's footsteps.

The sun was out and they all felt extremely safe because there was no way Mr Culard would be doing his rounds at this time. Tom picked his way along the special trail of stones and eventually they came to the mossy bank where he'd fallen asleep. The sweet smell of rotting leaves seeped up from their feet; the sun danced through the branches dappling them with its light and far away a pair of pigeons cooed and gurgled to each other.

Tom was amazed to remember how frightened he'd been the night before. With Miles and Susan horsing around as usual, Miles humming the odd snatch of a Eurythmics song, Susan joining in with the backing part, the sun dancing and the birds twittering, he almost wondered if he'd imagined his experiences of the night before. Surely there hadn't really been wolves here, where now there were coy robins hopping among the leaves; surely these steady, ancient trees, whose leaves formed an almost affectionate umbrella of luminous, golden trellis-work above them, couldn't be the same as those menacing pillars of blackness he'd seen the night before?

"So, what now?" said Susan, sitting down. "Do we just look around?"

"I guess so," said Tom. "I'll look to the north, you look to the south, Miles can look to the east and if none of us is lucky we'll go west together."

"And if we find nothing then we'll all go bonkers," said Miles.

They spent a good hour searching but with no results. Tom found a wrecked car, Miles unearthed a couple of dead rabbits and Susan discovered a tramp's hideout, but no coffins. Together they scouted to the west – but again with no luck. They sat down gloomily on a huge grass-covered hillock and munched some sandwiches that Miles had thoughtfully brought along.

"Just a wild goose-chase," said Tom. "All that effort wasted. It was probably just an ordinary bat. What wallies we are."

"Speak for yourself," said Susan, getting up and walking down the mound.

"Anyway, it's a nice day. And it's given us something to do."

"But it's frustrating," said Miles. "Now I know how they must feel when they're searching for the Yeti in the Himalayas."

"Heralayas," corrected Susan, from the bottom of the hillock. "Oh well, nothing ventured, nothing gained. Jeepers, it's pretty dank down here. And – hey, come and look!"

Tom and Miles scrambled down the mound to see what she was exclaiming about. There, fitted into the bottom of the hillock, were six iron bars pushed into the earth like the bars on a prison window and looking through they could see that the mound was hollow. Could something lurk inside?

"There can't be a coffin in there," said Miles, staring through the gloom. "Even Culard, thin as he is, couldn't squeeze through these bars. Nothing could."

"Except something small...like a bat," said Susan. "Hey, do you think he turns into a bat and flies in here, then flies out again and turns into Mr Culard? That must be it!"

"But how are we going to get in?" asked Miles, tugging at the bars. "There's no way we can shift these."

"What about at the side, if we dug some of this earth away?" suggested Tom, having a look. "We're small enough to squeeze in here if we were to make it bigger." And with the aid of a couple of sticks and a flat stone they managed to scrape away enough earth for them to wriggle through.

Inside it was very dark and damp. Drops of water dripped from the mossy ceiling onto the earth below and there was the rank smell of mould. Huge, flat, brown toadstools sprang from the sides of the cavern like great tables and a rat scurried across the floor making Susan jump.

The ground was black and slimy – no sunlight ever penetrated this cavern – and smelt of rotting flesh, as if animals had crawled in here to die. Their feet squelched as they walked further in and their faces brushed against dusty cobwebs which draped themselves from the roof. Tom could feel a spider crawling about in his hair and he gave an involuntary shake to get it free. He could feel the goose-pimples spring up on his arms and his hands started to shake.

"Anyone got a light?" asked Tom. Susan shook her head but Miles dug around in his pocket and produced a curious key with a light attached – no doubt something his father had given him.

Tom nervously fingered the garlic round his neck. "Come on, let's start looking," he suggested.

They had hardly gone any way into the back of the cavern when Miles stumbled over something. By the light of his tiny torch they could make it out. It was wooden, it was long and it was narrow. "It's a coffin!" breathed Susan. "It really is! Come on, guys, let's prise it open." Tom shrank back. Suddenly he wished he were back at school reading *The History of the Tele-*

phone. He had no wish to prise open anyone's coffin. Heaven only knew what they might find. It might be some rotting corpse. It might be a genuine dead person who'd be far from chuffed at having his coffin prised open by three schoolchildren. He turned to Miles apologetically but he was sitting down on the floor, his head between his knees.

"Sorry," he said, from down below. "Just feeling a bit faint. Must be the lack of air. I'll be OK in a minute. But I feel rather weak. I don't think I could prise open a coffin."

"No, I don't think we should," said Tom. He was starting to feel deeply afraid. "Isn't it against the laws of the church or something? We now know where the coffin is. Let's wait till Mr Fritz gets back and see what he says." He just wanted to get out of that place and back to the school as soon as possible. It was horribly creepy and dark in the cavern and he had an uneasy feeling that the bars might be bending back at this very moment, trapping them inside.

But Susan thought otherwise. "You two!" she said, irritably throwing back her frizzy red hair so it bounced all around her head. "We come here on a special coffin-prising expedition and when it comes to it you're both chicken. I'll simply have to do it myself, then."

She grabbed a huge stick that lay on the floor and started jabbing at the coffin furiously.

"Hey, not like that," said Miles, looking up, nervously. "You might wake him up. Anyway, you'll never get it open that way. You have to use a bit of intelligence."

"In that case," said Susan throwing down the stick angrily, "perhaps we had better look to Tom."

Eventually they found a flat piece of stone which they wedged under the top of the coffin and using all their strength they managed slowly to winch up the lid.

"It can't be the right coffin," said Tom, in the middle of it. "This coffin hasn't been opened in a hundred years."

"Stop making excuses," said Susan. "Here, let me have a go."

She then sat on the piece of stone and started bouncing up and down on it. Slowly the lid started to lift off, and as it did so, clouds of fetid dust poured from within. They all started coughing and spluttering but Susan continued.

The lid opened wider and wider, the wood splintering at the side with a sound like the crunching of old bones. Tiny, black insects, lodged for centuries in the oak, scuttled down the sides, onto the floor and over their shoes. There was a scraping, screaming sound as one of the two hinges twisted into action, the rust and mould spurting from the edges like sparks from a worn-out firework. As they pulled back the lid, a terrible smell of rot surged from the depths, forcing its way into their throats and nostrils as if it were trying to suffocate them. As it slowly diffused into the whole cave and as the dust cleared, they gazed down inside and Miles, with shaking hands, aimed his torch into the interior.

There, lying with its eyes closed and its arms crossed, was a body. A blood-stained piece of white material was wrapped around its head; its clothes looked remarkably familiar. Dirty, black shoes, wrinkled tight, black trousers, a greasy, black coat and, sticking out from filthy cuffs, gaunt, white fingers with long, grime-encrusted nails.

Susan looked at the boys as she nervously picked at the cloth that lay over the face.

"Shall I?" she asked. Her voice was trembling. They nodded. She pulled it swiftly away, and there, grinning up at them with red-rimmed eyes staring sightlessly ahead, was Mr Culard himself.

CHAPTER NINE

He didn't seem to be conscious. His skin was deathly pale and when Miles let a small leaf fall onto his half-open mouth, it didn't even waver. He just wasn't breathing. Miles gingerly placed Mr Culard's limp, bony wrist between his thumb and forefinger, a trick he'd picked up from his father's surgery. "He's cold as stone," he breathed, "and I can't feel a pulse at all."

As they stared at the body, a further stench rose up from the coffin – a smell of putrid, rotting flesh, mould and decay. Tom started back, holding his nose. "Ugh! Bakes school didders sbell like Chadel Dubber Five," he said. "Yuk!"

"He *must* be dead," said Miles as he gazed in. "He certainly isn't alive, anyway."

There was a long silence as they all looked down at the body.

"What shall we do?" said Susan. "Put the lid back on? Or shove some garlic in his mouth?"

"Both," said Tom, pulling the bulb of garlic from the string around his neck and placing it on Mr Culard's pointed teeth like a chef putting the finishing touch to a wedding cake. "That'll stop his activities for a while!"

"Why don't we get Mr Fox to come and see him?" suggested Susan. "Surely he'd believe us if he saw this? Then he could – um – get the police in or something."

"You must be crazy!" said Tom, rounding on her. "The police couldn't possibly cope with this, any more than they could deal with a nightmare! They can barely cope with common-or-garden psychotics. This'd blow their minds! I bet there's nothing about vampires in

English law, anyway. 'You can't loiter with intent or trespass on people's property or be drunk and disorderly,'" he said in a pompous voice, imitating a policeman. "'But being a vampire, that's fine. It's a free country and until laws about vampires are entered in the statute books, vampires are free to roam about as much as they like just as every other citizen of this land of democracy.' And there'd be no point in showing Mr Fox. He's mad enough as it is. He couldn't do anything, anyway."

But after some discussion, Miles agreed with Susan and, with two against one, Tom was forced to give in.

Sometimes they really irritated him. He would have thought it was obvious that no teacher – with the possible exception of Mr Fritz – could ever be trusted, least of all Mr Fox. Sometimes he felt they just saw all this as a jolly adventure – when he saw it as an issue of life and death. Obviously the fact that his father had been visited by Mr Culard made a difference – but it seemed to him that Miles and Susan didn't really understand the wider implications of Mr Culard's plans. It presumably wasn't just the school that Mr Culard was interested in – it must, eventually, be the whole world. Burlap Hall wasn't the be-all and end-all for him – it was just the first stepping stone of a master plan. Not only would the whole school become vampires but everyone's mums and dads – and his hamster and Errol and even Mrs Thatcher and Princess Di and Terry Wogan, Ian Botham and Frank Bruno and Stephen Spielberg. It was just too awful to think about.

When they'd put the coffin lid back in place and squeezed out of Mr Culard's tomb, he shambled after the other two disconsolately, worried and anxious about the whole situation. It would have been far better to have sealed up the coffin and just gone away and left it, as Mr Fritz had told them. Then when Mr Fritz came back they would have been really one-up on Mr Culard. Now they were going to blow everything. He looked anxiously at the bright sky and then at his watch. It was one o'clock. There'd be no way Mr Culard could get up now, but it started to get dark around 4.45 p.m. They didn't have a lot of time.

Mr Fox was just starting his lunch when they returned. He was irritated that they should interrupt him in the middle of a delicious prawn vol-au-vent he had driven all the way in to Lanchester to buy from his favourite delicatessen. Not to mention the glass of chilled white wine he'd just poured himself. That was the big advantage of half-term and the holidays. He could use the school fridge to chill his drinks – while in term time he thought it might not be *comme il faut*.

"I'll have a word with you later," he said rather grandly, wiping a prawn away from his upper lip with his napkin. "Just leave me be for half an hour or so. I've got a lot of work to catch up on." And with that he returned to the copy of the *Sun* he had hidden in *The Daily Telegraph*.

The hours seemed to drag ever so slowly for the children as they waited. They ate their lunch in about three minutes and then just hung around the Common Room, waiting for Mr Fox to summon them. Miles tried to start a game of chess but none of them could concentrate. The only thing that was in their minds was the haggard face of Mr Culard, staring up at them from his coffin with his dead, blood-shot eyes, his washed-out complexion, a ghastly contrast to his

134

bright, red, scabbed lips.

It was 3.30 before Mr Fox called them and when they arrived in his office the phone rang and he talked for what seemed like hours with some supplier of textbooks, haggling over the price.

By the time he turned to them and asked them what they wanted to talk about, it was 3.45. And none of them knew how to start the discussion.

"It's about – er, Mr Culard," said Susan, nervously.

"Well, not so much Mr Culard as – er, vampires," interrupted Miles.

Tom stared miserably at the crumbs from the prawn vol-au-vent which were scattered on the floor. He knew they shouldn't have told Mr Fox. It was a big mistake.

As Miles and Susan unfolded the story Mr Fox became more and more incredulous.

"He turned into a *what*?" he fumed when they told him about Mr Culard's capacity for transforming himself into a bat. "You *what*?" he exploded when they told him about sprinkling the flour round Miss Shepherd – but his explosion was more to cover up an irresistible giggle that had wriggled up inside him when he imagined the situation. And finally, "*What* a load of rubbish!" he burst out, at the end of the saga.

And yet. And yet. Secretly, inside himself, Mr Fox wondered. Could it possibly, possibly be that the children's story contained a grain of truth? It certainly would account for all the uncanny happenings at Burlap Hall that term. And Mr Culard *was* the most fearfully sinister-looking figure. And he remembered what the teachers had said about mirrors when he'd upbraided them about their appearance. And what Mrs Grain had said about running water. And of course he'd seen Signor Ruzzi's bizarre behaviour in church for himself. He would never admit to the children in a hundred years that he thought their story was other than complete piffle, but it interested him more than they realized.

"Well, come along, then, let's see this so-called coffin of yours!" he said, breezily, getting up. "I could do with a walk, wild goose-chase or no wild goose-chase!"

"But, sir, it's very late," cried Tom. "He may have got up by now! Even though we did put garlic in his mouth!"

"Nonsense! Mr Culard never teaches till 5.00. I should know. I do the timetables, after all. Come along! And I hope this isn't all some stupid prank because if so, there'll be trouble! Half-term or no half-term!" He bent down to put on the shoes he'd comfortably kicked off under the table while having lunch and, seeing a rogue prawn on the carpet, popped it into his mouth. Delicious! Next time he must buy two vol-au-vent, at least.

He walked to the door of his office and flung it open – only to surprise Mr Carstairs who was crouching down outside.

"Carstairs! What are you doing here?" he asked in amazement. A look established itself on his face without his even summoning it.

"Oh, just tying my shoelaces – sorry, Mr Fox," mumbled Mr Carstairs, straightening up with a guilty expression on his face. "I'm just off on my run."

"And where are you going today?" asked Mr Fox, suspiciously.

"I'm going six times round the lawn as usual," said Mr Carstairs – but he surprised himself as he said it. His Master had just spoken to him, asking for his presence in the woods down by the crossroads; he'd told him to get there quickly because he was in trouble. But why was Carstairs unable to tell Mr Fox? He couldn't understand. He opened his mouth to explain but nothing came out except a repetition of his former lie. "I'm going six times round the lawn as usual."

"Well, we're going down to the woods by the cross-roads on a wild goose-chase," snorted Mr Fox. "Come and have a sherry later on, Carstairs. I want to discuss this idea you have for getting 2C to study Dostoevsky's *Notes from the House of the Dead*. I'm not sure I'm in favour. I thought that for this half of the term you were doing Wordsworth."

So did Mr Carstairs, but so many odd things had happened recently he didn't know whether he was coming or going. He grunted a reply and darted off.

"He's another one," said Miles, pointing at Carstairs' vanishing figure. "He *would* want to do a book like that now that Mr Culard's got to him."

"Nonsense!" snapped Mr Fox, striding forward. But inside he wondered if Miles couldn't be right.

It certainly wasn't as light as before when they got to the village at 4.20. Tom just hoped that the garlic had hindered Mr Culard in some way, but he feared the worst. Particularly as he'd spotted Mr Carstairs in his green tracksuit darting over the fields in the direction of the wood.

"It's too late! Mr Culard will have got up by now!" said Tom, and Miles and Susan knew he had a point. But Mr Fox would have none of it.

"You can't make an accusation and then not carry it through!" he said tersely. "If you make an accusation you've got to be prepared to stand by that accusation." But deep down he was longing to see if Mr Culard actually *was* lying in his coffin in the wood.

They ploughed through the trees, now quite familiar with the route. Mr Fox huffed and puffed, unused to all this exercise, and the sticks and leaves under his feet made a fearful racket as he tramped ahead. Eventually they arrived at the hillock.

"How's he going to get in?" whispered Miles to Tom, pointing at Mr Fox's rotund figure. "He'll never squeeze through those bars."

"We'll just have to do some more digging," groaned Tom. "That'll delay us even more."

Mr Fox peered suspiciously at the dark interior through the bars. Then he gave a startled shout.

"What is it, sir?" asked Tom.

"Nothing, nothing, just a bird," said Mr Fox, brushing his cheek in an irritated way. But in fact he'd been thoroughly shaken by the experience of fluttering wings against his face. "Well, where now?"

They managed to dig a space wide enough for Mr Fox to get through and it was 4.45 by the time they finally assembled in the hollow mausoleum.

"Look, look, it's still there!" cried Susan, pointing to the coffin. "And it's still shut. He must be there!"

They found their piece of stone and, for the second time that day, they forced open the lid of the coffin.

"Look, look!" shouted Miles, seizing Mr Fox's arm and pointing as the lid started to open. But there was a horrible surprise in store. As the lid creaked upwards they could see things had changed since they had been there that morning.

"Oh, my goodness!" shrieked Susan, as the lid creaked up. "He's not there!"

A terrible silence fell on them as they all peered into the coffin. It was true. It was completely empty. There was some torn red silk, the blood-stained cloth, a couple of old twigs – and nothing else at all. They stood there, stunned, unable to speak. Then their silence was interrupted. A terrible and familiar voice, droning and hypnotic, came echoing into the mausoleum.

"*Who* is not *where*?"

They turned and there, standing on the other side of the bars, in the shadow of the now-darkening wood, staring in, was Mr Culard. Behind him, a horrible smirk on his face, was Mr Carstairs in his tracksuit, sweating slightly and rubbing his hands.

Tom was the first to speak with an excited rush of words. "Don't you see, sir, it's him. Mr Carstairs helped him to change into a bat and fly out, that was what you felt on your face, Mr Culard flying out! It's true, everything we said is true, I promise you, sir!"

Mr Fox scratched his head. It certainly sounded true, but on the other hand...why the devil did Mr Culard keep staring at him like that? His eyes seemed to have turned into great, glowing circles, hypnotizing him. Try as he might to blink, his eyelids refused to obey. He could do nothing but stare back, mesmerized, into Mr Culard's eyes.

"You don't believe them, do you, Mr Fox?" droned Mr Culard, his voice soft and monotonous. "You know they aren't speaking the truth. They are naughty children, up to foolish pranks. You are a sensible man, aren't you? You have a mind of your own."

Mr Fox wondered if he *did* have a mind of his own at this particular juncture, particularly when he heard himself repeating Mr Culard's words back to him like a parrot. "I don't believe them, I know they are not speaking the truth," he heard himself say, his voice slurred and indistinct. "They are naughty children, up to foolish pranks. I am a sensible man. I have a mind of my own."

"Sir, sir, he's hypnotizing you, can't you see?" pleaded Susan, tugging at his sleeve.

But Mr Culard would not release Mr Fox from his stare. "I am not hypnotizing you, am I, Mr Fox? I am talking good, sound sense. These children must be punished even though it is still half-term. They must have a detention. A detention given them by me, by Mr Culard."

Mr Fox stared blindly ahead. "You are not hypnotizing me. You are talking good, sound sense. These children must be punished even though it is still half-term. They must have a detention. A detention given them by you, Mr Culard."

"Thank you kindly, dear Mr Fox," said Mr Culard in a more normal voice as he helped him out through the gap in the railings, "for entrusting me with the very onerous task of punishing these children. Please go on ahead and I will follow with the culprits. They will be punished severely not only for wasting your time but also for casting a slur on my good name!" And with a bemused nod of his head, Mr Fox allowed himself to be led ahead by Mr Carstairs through the wood.

The children looked at each other as they saw his vanishing figure. Was there any way of escape? Mr Culard stood at the entrance by the bars, preventing their exit.

"I have all the time in the world, my dears," he said, cunningly. "There is no escape. This way, please."

Miles gave a last desperate look around and then tried to rush him at the entrance. But as he hurtled towards Mr Culard and knocked into him, hard enough to make most people fall over, Mr Culard just gave a sly smile. Miles fell at his feet as if he'd rushed into a brick wall and stumbled up, rubbing his head.

"I wouldn't try that. I am a lot stronger than you. I have special powers," smiled Mr Culard. "Susan, my dear, ladies first. Come to me — your good teacher — Mr A. Culard."

Reluctantly Susan shuffled towards the entrance and when she came within reaching distance of Mr Culard he shot his arm forward like a snake and clasped her arm in an iron grip, pulling her viciously towards him.

"Ow! Stop that!" screamed Susan as he dragged her outside. "Anyway, your name isn't Mr Culard! You know what your name is. It's Count Dracula!"

"May I present my compliments, Madame," said Mr Culard, bowing low but still holding her tightly. "I am glad you like the name. For soon," he added with a hyena-like laugh, "we will share the name — when I make you my bride!"

"Bride? Bride? You must be joking!" snapped Susan. "I'm never going to marry anyone, least of all an old bat like you!"

"I think you will be changing your mind very soon," murmured Mr Culard as he gripped her arm harder, guiding her through the wood. "What a very pretty neck you have, my dear. I had never noticed it before. And I am glad we have a couple of slaves to help at the ceremony," he added pointing at Miles and Tom. "I like a bride to bring a retinue with her. It makes the bridal breakfast so much more — succulent."

"What are we going to do?" whispered Miles to Tom, as he ducked under the branch of a tree. "I'm scared stiff!"

"I'd say we should make a run for it, but then we'd be leaving Susan," whispered Tom. "But there are three of us and only one of him. He can't hypnotize us all at the same time. We'll have to gang up and if he concentrates on one of us, the others must say the Lord's Prayer at him like mad!"

"Well, at least Susan's got her cross round her neck. She should be OK. And we've got a bit of garlic each." said Miles. "That'll protect us up to a point."

"Thank goodness," said Tom, putting his hand up to his neck to feel the comforting bulb. But there was nothing there. He rummaged frantically around in his pocket. His hand felt a penknife, a bit of chewed chewing-gum wrapped up in a piece of silver paper waiting for a second session, the rubber he'd never returned to Asquith Minor, a broken key-ring, a scrap of paper on which he'd done rather a brilliant cartoon of Signor Ruzzi playing the piano – but, horror of horrors, no garlic. Not so much as a clove. Then he remembered. He'd stuffed it into Mr Culard's mouth in the coffin. He must have been mad. He was now completely unprotected. "I haven't got it any more! I put it in Culard's mouth!" he gasped.

"Isn't there anything back at the school you could use? A couple of rulers tied into a cross?" whispered Miles, worriedly.

"No, detention's always in the gym, now, and I can't go scouring the school for rulers." Then a thought hit him. As they got through the main door of the school, Mr Fox was waiting for them and Tom surprised both him and Mr Culard by shooting up his hand and saying, "Please, sir, before detention, may I use the toilet, please?"

And before Mr Culard had time to organize any hypnotism tricks, Mr Fox had said, "Very well, but make it snappy!" and Tom darted off in the direction of his bedroom.

The Bible! That's what he'd remembered. He hauled his suitcase from under the bed and rummaged through. No sign of it anywhere. He could have sworn he had packed it in the end. But where could it be? He scoured his bookcase but it wasn't to be seen. Then he remembered. He'd used it as one of a pile to prop up the side of his bed which had collapsed when he and Miles had a pillow-fight one night. He pulled it out, stuffed it under his jumper and raced downstairs.

"A half-hour detention is needed," said Mr Culard to Mr Fox, staring at him intently. "I think that will suit my purposes."

"A half-hour detention," repeated Mr Fox, "to suit your purposes." He felt mighty queer. He ought to go up to his study to have a drink. What *was* happening to Burlap Hall this term? He turned on his heel and made his way unsteadily up the stairs.

Inside the gym Mr Culard motioned for the three children to sit down while he carefully checked the locks on the doors.

"I don't want to take any risks, my dears," he said, chuckling slightly to himself as he walked around rattling at the locks with his bony fingers.

"I think we are secure," he said, coming to sit down in front of them.

"Perhaps I had better explain. Although there is obviously not a lot to explain since you clearly know so much. A bright little bunch you are, aren't you? And yet," he added, leaning foward and breathing on them with his fetid breath, "no one is too bright to become the servant of Count Dracula, Prince of Darkness."

"You fiend!" hissed Miles. "If you just want us dead, why don't you just kill us?"

"My dear Miles, if only it were as easy as that!"

143

exclaimed Mr Culard with a hideous smile. "If I just wanted all of you dead I should have put a bomb under the school long ago. Ah...to die...to be really dead...that must be glorious!" He looked wistfully into the middle distance.

"But I am afraid there are far worse things awaiting man than death — as you yourselves will discover all too soon, my dears. My plan is to take over the entire school — and then, when I have Burlap Hall in my power, we shall all go forth and conquer the world!

"By the way," he added turning his hooded eyes to Tom, "I had an interesting talk with your father recently who told me of his hopes that you should have a good career when you are older. Little does he know, the dear man, that you will never get any older; and little does he also know that I have already marked out a glorious career for you — as my servant! Though after our little chat he may be starting to have faint glimmerings!" Mr Culard gave a horrible chuckle.

"However, time is running short. We can't delay." He turned and looked the three of them up and down and finally his gaze settled on Miles. "To begin, I shall choose you, my dear Miles, as the first of my servants. You will learn all the ways of blood and darkness. You will be able to help me instruct your friends. And soon your teeth will grow long and white, like mine." And he smiled viciously, revealing two razor-sharp fangs glistening against his bright red lips.

"No luck," said Miles, bravely. "I've got a brace which my parents have told me has got to stay on for two years, so ner!"

"I don't think your parents will have much influence over your decisions in the future," said Mr Culard, giving a grating chuckle. He got up slowly and with three deadly steps approached Miles with his teeth bared; he stretched out to grab at his shoulders. Miles immediately held up his bulb of garlic and Mr Culard gave a hiss of revulsion and started away.

"So! You wish to cheat me! Very well. But I will defeat you in the end. I will get your friend and then together we will overpower you!"

Crouching low like a wild animal, he turned to Tom and as he approached with twisted, hopping steps, Tom could smell his rank breath. His white teeth dazzled Tom and his eyes were bright and fascinating, compelling him to stare and stare for an eternity. For a moment Tom was almost tempted to give in — but then he tugged the Bible down from under his jersey and held it up in front of his face.

Mr Culard shot into a corner with a scream, shuddering with hatred. "Foiled again!" he hissed. "But wait! I will gather my psychic forces! I'll take the girl! And you shall be witnesses at our wedding!"

He muttered an incantation to himself and started to approach Susan. Miles held up his garlic and though Mr Culard flinched, it didn't seem to deter him as it had done before. Tom pushed his Bible under his nose but, giving a howl of pain, Mr Culard flung out an arm and dashed it to the ground. "Wretched book, be gone!" he shrieked. His dank red hair was wildly out of place now, starting out from his head in mad strands and his eyes gleamed like gas burners.

He moved closer and closer to Susan. "My red-haired bride! You will be mine! Together we will roam the earth, for ever and ever, seeking fresh blood!"

"Susan, get out your crucifix!" yelled Tom and Miles. And then they both started yelling at the top of their voices: "Our Father which art in Heaven . . ."

145

Susan pulled up her crucifix and Mr Culard cowered, twitching slightly "I shall reassemble my forces," he howled. "My children, my servants! Come to me!" And suddenly, through the bars of the windows in the gym, came an enormous colony of bats, fluttering through the air till it was dark with their wings. Tom started to feel dizzy. "Hallowed be Thy name!" he was yelling, but his voice seemed to be getting fainter and fainter. "Thy kingdom come, Thy will be done..." But his voice was too hoarse. His throat seemed to be full of bats. At the other side of the room he saw Miles slump down as if he'd been knocked out by an invisible fist. And Mr Culard, surrounded by bats, was hovering over Susan, baring his white teeth over her exposed neck with a low, growling noise as if saliva was boiling in his evil throat.

Then there was a hammering on the door.

"Open up in there! In the name of the Lord! *Kanti Kanti, el maranti, Jextapus sholem, vixit, vixit!*"

It was the voice of Mr Fritz and at the sound of this incantation Mr Culard went even whiter than he was already.

He drew back from Susan like a frightened animal. "So! Your scientific friend has discovered the words! But they won't protect him for long, you'll see! Tomorrow night you will be my bride! Till then, my dear!"

Mr Fritz was thundering at the door, putting his

shoulder to it, and Tom could see it bulging at each blow. In a second it would break.

Mr Culard, a furious, distorted shape in the middle of the room, suddenly shrivelled into a small black object which fluttered on the floor. Before their eyes, he changed into a bat, rose up and, with all the other bats, flew out of the window. At the same time Mr Fritz burst in.

CHAPTER TEN

Very slowly Tom felt his circulation, which fear had paralysed, returning to his body. He pulled himself up from where he had fallen and balanced himself with one hand on a desk. He felt extremely wobbly and the room seemed to be whirling around him.

"Sit down, Buxton!" instructed Mr Fritz. "Put your head between your knees so the blood can get to your brain! Otherwise you'll only faint. And that goes for you two as well," he added, turning to Miles and Susan who were both trying rather unsuccessfully to stagger up from the floor. "What a narrow escape!" he said, shaking his head.

"Don't you think *you'd* better get some blood to your brain as well?" said Tom, who was feeling much better as he cradled his head on his knees. "We don't want you passing out at this stage, sir."

"Good idea," said Mr Fritz, getting down onto the floor and sticking his head down as well. The hairs on his hairy suit tickled his eyebrows and he sneezed. In a few minutes they had all recovered their composure and the children were eagerly begging Mr Fritz to tell them what he'd discovered in Romania.

"A lot," he replied, sitting on the vaulting horse and getting out a notebook. "A lot of very useful stuff indeed, as has already been demonstrated. I learnt that chant from an old woodcutter who lives near the forest and is a renowned expert in vampires. Of course the chant won't kill Mr Culard and he will be able to assemble powers to defeat it eventually, but it's useful to know in an emergency. For your information it goes like this." He looked at his notebook and checked the words. "In the name of the Lord! *Kanti Kanti, el maranti, Jextapus sholem, vixit, vixit!*"

They all tried it out and managed to learn it by heart. "Sounds like those words Mr Fox wins with in Scrabble," said Miles, gloomily.

"But I have learnt other things as well. Namely" – and he put his notebook back in his pocket – "how to destroy Mr Culard and, by destroying him, free the other teachers of the fatal spell they are under. How's Mr Fox, by the way? I saw him when I got in and he seemed to be raving on about having been hypnotized by Mr Culard and how he was a vampire. How would he know? What's been happening?"

Tom, Miles and Susan recounted to Mr Fritz all their adventures and he listened, nodding wisely all the time.

"You've been extremely brave, you know," he said, finally, getting out his pipe and tapping it. "Brave to the point of foolhardiness, if you don't mind my saying so. And it is of course a shame that Mr Culard realizes you've found his coffin because obviously he will be moving his hiding-place at the earliest opportunity. However, there's nothing that can be done about it now. What we must discuss is his destruction."

The children all wriggled closer to listen, sitting cross-legged on the gym floor.

"There are several ways of killing a vampire and I think we should discuss each option in turn. First, driving a stake through his heart."

"Ugh, no thanks," said Tom. "I'd rather die."

"Well, that may be your only alternative, Tom," said Mr Fritz giving a grim smile. "But I agree. Too messy. And, as we discussed, there's the chance of being wrongly convicted of murder. He could be burnt alive...but I think the same disadvantages apply. On the other hand we could shoot him through the heart with a silver bullet that has been blessed by a priest. But even assuming we had a gun and desired to shoot Mr Culard, getting a silver bullet would be a problem and I can't see the vicar blessing it without asking a few embarrassing questions. And shooting him through the heart precisely would prove even harder, since as far as I know none of us is an expert marksman." At a furious look from Susan he apologetically added: "Or markswoman."

"However," he continued, "there is one other option that I have discovered and it sounds to me as if this may be our answer. My woodcutter friend told me that if, when a vampire is transformed into something small like, say, a bat, he is trapped in a bottle and then burnt, he would be destroyed for ever. Now this would neatly solve our problem. We could not be had up for murder because we would have only destroyed a bat."

"But isn't it illegal to destroy bats? And anyway, isn't it a fine point – we know it's Mr Culard. We really are killing him!" protested Susan, who was getting anxious.

"Frankly, my dear, we could be here till next Wednesday discussing the philosphical ins and outs of this problem. Is the bat Mr Culard? Is Mr Culard the bat? When Mr Culard is acting as Mr Culard, is he also a bat? When the bat is acting like a bat, is it also Mr Culard? Soon you'll be asking me whether this vaulting horse really exists when we all leave the room. Or if it isn't a figment of our combined imaginations."

Miles looked at Tom in a puzzled way and whispered: "What's he on about? Of course it'll still be a vaulting horse!"

"I heard that, Miles!" said Mr Fritz, smiling slightly. "You agree with me – and Gertrude Stein – that a bat is a bat is a bat. Just so. Which is why we must kill it."

Miles looked even more baffled and muttered: "Gertrude who?" but didn't attempt to argue.

"Now, what I am wondering is – should we bring Mr Fox in on all this? Ought we give him the chance to protect himself? I have to say he seemed half convinced – but he's such an erratic man. He might hinder us more than help us. But perhaps we need all the allies we can get in this difficult time. Half-term ends tonight and it'll be back to normal school tomorrow. And Mr Culard is bound to strike again soon."

"Let's sleep on it," suggested Susan. "So much has happened today I can't think straight. But in the meantime – how are we going to lure Mr Culard into a bottle? I mean lure the bat into the bottle?"

"I've wondered about that," said Mr Fritz, stroking his chin. "We need two kinds of bait. First is the bait for Mr Culard, and second is the bait for the bat."

"Of course," said Susan. "But what sort of bat are you thinking of for Mr Culard – and what sort of bat for the bait? I mean...what sort of bait for the bait – er, bat for the bat – oh, hell, I can't get it right."

"For the bat it's quite easy. A delicious fly? A juicy cockroach? Some kind of insect, anyway. For Mr Culard it's more difficult. I hate to say it, but what about you, Susan? Obviously we'd all be in the room with you, but hidden."

"*Me*?" exploded Susan. "Why me? Just because I'm a girl. Jeepers! I think that's a bit much."

"It's not our fault that Mr Culard is sexist," said Miles, "or that he fancies you. It's just that vampires like beautiful young virgins." And he gave an awful leering laugh which made Susan deliver him a look sizzling with fury.

"Nuts! You're just winding me up!" she snapped. "I'm not going to be bait for Mr Culard! You must be joking! Anyway, what about Rosemary? She'll be there as well, remember!"

"Don't worry about Rosemary," said Tom. "She's coming back two days late because she's got a ballet performance at home. She told me."

"Susan, there will be no chance at all of your being hurt," said Mr Fritz. "You must know that we would all protect you. It's just a matter of choosing the one among us who is the most attractive to Mr Culard, the one who will lure him in the quickest. If I thought that I would be remotely tempting, I would offer myself. I am much older than you, I've lived a long time and death holds no terrors for me. Please trust me. We all have our parts to play and each of them is just as dangerous as the others. We're all in this together."

"All right," grumbled Susan. "Only if something happens to me . . ."

"Nothing will happen to you," Mr Fritz assured her, tapping his pipe. "You have nothing to fear. And now," he added, looking at his watch, "we must go our separate ways. But tomorrow night, when everyone is back from half-term, we should perhaps think of putting this plan into action. The sooner we can release Burlap Hall from the terror which grips it, the batter. I mean," he added irritably, "better."

That night Mr Fox, clad in a striped nightshirt, tossed and turned uneasily in his bed. Apart from all that vampire business he'd had an enjoyable rest at half-term and he dreaded the start of school again the following day. The Sleepeezie mattress didn't seem to be working its usual magic either. To make things worse there was an awful howling noise outside like a wolf – but that must be his imagination. Could it be that he, too, was finally going down with the bug that seemed to have attacked everyone else? And yet it wasn't so much that he felt ill, it was more...well, he had to face it. It was Mr Culard. He couldn't stop thinking about the way he'd looked at him in the wood. And it was his eyes, in particular, that he couldn't drive from his mind. In a way they were comforting, but in another way they were terrifying, and Mr Fox couldn't decide which...

With a great wrench of his mind he tried to concentrate on the facts. Fact One: Mr Culard *looked* like a vampire. But that wouldn't stand up in court. Fact Two: all the teachers seemed to be turning into creatures that had certain similarities with vampires (i.e. hatred of mirrors, running water, daylight). Fact Three: what had that coffin been doing in the wood? Another part of Mr Fox got a bit angry about this, pointing out that it wasn't a fact, just a question, so he re-phrased it to himself: Fact Three: there was a coffin in the wood. Fact Four: a bat had flown out through the bars and Mr Culard had appeared from nowhere. Fact Five: Mr Fritz, just returned from Romania, had rushed into the gym chanting a fearful incantation and there was no sign of Mr Culard when Mr Fox had looked in afterwards. There had been nothing in the gym except, oddly, an inordinate number of bat-droppings. Fact Five: (or had he already had fact five?) He started to go over the Facts in his mind but counting Facts had the same effect as counting sheep and he soon fell into a deep sleep. And it was when he was asleep that he had

153

the most scary dream he'd ever had.

He dreamt he was lying in bed in the
middle of the night when there was
a scratching at the window. He'd
tried to ignore it but it became so
persistent that he had got up
and gone over to the window
– and lo and behold – who
should be out there, staring in,
but Mr Culard!

"Let me in!" Mr Culard
had intoned, in such a
loud voice that Mr Fox
was certain that he'd
wake the whole school.

"For heaven's sake, man, keep your voice down," he
whispered furiously. "There are people sleeping here!
Have more consideration for others!"

"I am your Master," droned Mr Culard, his hot
breath misting up the window. "Let me in!"

"I'm sorry: you may be *a* master, but you're not *my*
master. I am the headmaster in this school and I'll
thank you to remember it," replied Mr Fox, peevishly.
"Go home at once to your lodgings in the village. And
anyway," he added, waking up a bit, "how do you
come to be looking in at my window? My bedroom is
on the third floor!"

"I am your Master!" replied Mr Culard. "Let me in!
Let me in!"

In order to make his point by repeating what he'd
said before, Mr Fox made the big mistake of looking
directly into Mr Culard's glowing red eyes. Like gleaming magnets they held him transfixed: he felt that by
looking into them long enough he would discover the

secret of the universe. There was no question of ticking him off for making a racket; rather the opposite. He felt that Mr Culard had complete power over him whether he liked it or not.

Despite himself his hands reached out to the bottom of the window; it made a squeaking, creaking sound like pain as he slowly lifted it up to let Mr Culard into his room.

Assembly was held later than usual the next day to make time for all the arrivals back from half-term. Most of the pupils and teachers had arrived on the early train, to make the most of their holiday. It seemed that Asquith Minor had been to the States *twice* in one week by Concorde which seemed a bit much to Tom who had only ever been as far as Boulogne on a day-trip and that was when he was eighteen months old and he had no memory of it whatsoever. There was a photograph to prove it, however, of his mother on a boat holding a small, white bundle that she assured him was him as a baby, though Tom had his doubts. It looked more like a poodle, but she'd carefully explained it couldn't have been a poodle because of the rabies' laws.

Various other boys and girls had been to far-flung exotic places and Tom envied them their adventures – though he reminded himself that even if they'd been round the world a hundred times in the last seven days, none of their adventures could match his own experiences during the holiday.

Though really he'd have preferred just going home and sitting in front of the fire and reading his copies of *Smash Hits*. His mother would have bought him some chocolate rolls and Jaffacakes and he would have made one of his special milk-shakes with two different colours of ice-cream and maybe he'd have watched *Wogan* and *Dempsey and Makepeace*, followed by a long relaxing bath listening to Janice Long on the radio...then tried out that new black writing paper by sending a letter to his cousin written in white and decorating the envelope...there were far better things to do than go abroad. However, going home was a long way off, another six weeks to be exact. And who knew, if Mr Culard had his way, whether there would be any kind of home to go home to. Probably his home in future would be just a coffin in the woods. Certainly no telly. It was an awful prospect.

As the pupils filtered into the hall for assembly, everyone was chattering about what they'd been doing; but they quietened down when Mr Fox mounted the platform and gave a loud cough to announce his presence.

"Welcome, boys and girls, to the second half of the winter term," he said, in a confident, resonant voice. "And welcome, too, to a new regime that I hope will be to your liking." He ran his eye over the list he held in one hand.

"I have had much time for thought over the halfterm and I have come to realize that although there are many things to be recommended at Burlap Hall, nothing is so perfect as can do without improvement. And there are many ways to implement that improvement."

Tom looked at Miles and they both made faces at each other. Probably some cracked new penny-pinching wheeze for the monitors to do the washing-up, or for everyone to get up an hour earlier than usual.

Mr Fox put both his hands on the sides of his gown

and pulled them downwards in a pompous way. "Number One: We are going to put the day back considerably. For the rest of this term no one will rise before 5.00 p.m. in the afternoon and lessons will be conducted throughout the night. The evening meal will be served at 3.00 a.m. in the morning. The only exception will be the next two days since I know that you will need to accustom yourselves to this new regime. Tonight you will all put your lights out at 11.30 p.m. Tomorrow at 2.00 a.m. And the next day at 5.00 a.m."

There was a general surprised muttering from the pupils and faint giggles all round. Still, everyone seemed rather to relish the idea of going to bed and getting up so late.

"Number Two: I have decided to stop our water supply. It is too expensive and the money saved will be used in other ways. Anyone who is thirsty can drink bottled water, which will be in plentiful supply as I have just ordered a hundred cases."

There were even more murmurings – and mutters of "No baths? Great!" round the hall.

"It has also been brought to my notice that several of you are becoming very vain and as a punishment I am forbidding the possession of all mirrors for the rest of the term. Anyone found with a mirror on his or her person or in his or her room will be subject to three detentions."

"Always his or her, with his first," complained Susan. "Never her or his."

"I have also, after deep thought," continued Mr Fox, "decided that religious education is a waste of time, not to mention your parents' money. That is why I am abolishing it from now on. Anyone who wishes to attend church attends at their peril. As a result, Bibles, crosses or any other bits of religious paraphernalia will be viewed with much disfavour.

"And finally, garlic. I have heard that there are some among you, whose names shall be nameless" (whoops, there I go again, thought Mr Fox) "who have been *hoarding* garlic in their rooms. This is forbidden from now onwards. Is that quite clear?"

And as he opened his mouth to deliver a reassuring grin to the whole school, he revealed his teeth. And in particular, two long, white, pointed fangs at each side of his mouth.

CHAPTER ELEVEN

"Tonight. At midnight. Susan's room," whispered Mr Fritz to Tom, Miles and Susan. He was the first teacher to leave the hall and looked sick with worry. Even the hairs on his hairy suit seemed to be standing on end with anxiety. Tom, Miles and Susan nodded, silent with fear.

The other teachers followed, more relaxed and depraved than ever. Mrs Grain passed them, howling with mad laughter as her bun came unfastened and her dirty hair cascaded down her back; Miss Shepherd covered her lips with her hand as she giggled in response – as if she didn't want anyone to see her teeth. Mr Roy and Mr Carstairs, arm in arm, were involved in deep conspiratorial whispers and Signor Ruzzi had donned a large, black cloak which flapped dismally as he strode down the aisle, a wild look in his eyes.

As he passed the children he gave a faint sniff, then held up his hand.

"Garleec!" he announced. "I smell garleec!"

"All right, all right," said Mr Fox, pushing his way up to the front. "Where is it? Who's got it?" He came close to the three children, sniffing and snorting like an animal.

"Not just garlic but crucifixes!" he shrieked as he came closer to Susan. "I thought I'd told you crucifixes were forbidden! I can tell you've got one round your neck, I can just tell! You'll be punished! Maximus pessimissimus punishimus! Give it to me!"

Susan shrank away but then reluctantly hauled up the chain from the front of her blouse. Slowly she

159

unfastened it and then, smiling slightly, she held it out
to him.

"Perhaps you'd like to take it, sir?" she said, challen-
gingly. Mr Fox leant forward to snatch it from her
hand but the minute he came close to the chain, he
started away as if he'd been hit by an electric volt.

"Drop it, girl, drop it where you are!" he howled. "I
don't want to touch it!"

But Susan simply held it out, advancing on him as he
retreated.

"Asquith Minor!" yelled Mr Fox, spotting him nearby. "Take it from her! Do as I say!"

And before she knew what he'd done, Asquith
Minor had reached over and snatched it away.

"It's only a silly old crucifix," he muttered apologetically. "And you never go to church. And I don't
want to get detention even if you do."

"Now, take it to the toilet and flush it down the
lavatory! At once!" Mr Fox's voice was loud and
piercing.

Asquith Minor looked surprised but then he said:
"But, sir, I thought you said there was no running
water?"

Mr Fox snarled angrily. "Correct! Throw it out of
the window! At once!"

Tom and Miles leapt forward to stop him, but Asquith Minor was too quick for them. The crucifix flew
out of the window to be lost in a clump of bushes
below.

"You big idiot!" whispered Tom. "You big nerd-
face! Der-brain! Wally cubed! Fart-breath! Standing
toad-pool! Bong-tucker!" he added, running out of
insults but thinking that "bong-tucker" *sounded* pretty
insulting even if he didn't have a clue what it meant.

Asquith Minor looked suitably ashamed and backed into a crowd of pupils who were all giggling nervously.

"Now that's better," said Mr Fox. "But I can still smell garlic! All right, Buxton. Own up!"

Tom turned out his pockets with an air of innocence, aware all the time of a munching sound from Miles. He turned to look at him and saw his face was red and sweating as he chewed, as if he were eating something disgusting.

"Parker! It must be you with the garlic, then," said Mr Fox, turning to him in a fury.

But Miles put his face very close to Mr Fox's and, opening his mouth as wide as he could, he breathed: "No, sir!"

At the smell of Miles' garlicky breath Mr Fox reeled back as if he'd been hit on the nose by a cannonball.

"Ah, well, that smell will soon wear off," he said, as he was helped upright by Mrs Grain and Mr Carstairs. "And then we shall see about what we shall see about.

"Now, what's the time? Half past seven. Time for supper, a nice meaty supper, I think. A soup of meat stock, followed by roast meat and some blood oranges for pudding! Very tasty! Yum! Yum! Yum!"

After supper Tom, Miles and Susan rushed off to Mr Fritz's room. To their horror they found it devoid of garlic or crosses and Mr Fritz, looking very fed up, was fiddling about with a jar, a tube of glue and a bit of wire.

"Mr Fox gave orders for some of the children to strip all the rooms of garlic, Bibles, mirrors and so on during supper," he said, gloomily. "Now we're all unprotected."

"I think my Bible's safe, sir," said Tom, remembering he had put it back to prop up the bed. "I don't think anyone would look there."

Mr Fritz cheered up. "Excellent!" he said. "That's something, at least! I hope it's a nice big one, not a measly pocket one."

"Quite big, sir, but not enough for all three of us, I shouldn't think."

"You never know. The Bible's a very powerful book," said Mr Fritz, thoughtfully. "But in the meantime, can any of you help me with this? You've got smaller fingers than I have."

"Let's see," said Miles, leaning forward.

"Phew!" said Mr Fritz leaning back. "What a dreadful smell of garlic! Or perhaps I should say 'delicious' in the circumstances. Have you been eating it?"

"Yes, sir," said Miles, grinning. "And because of my brace I've still got lots of yukky bits lodged in the wire, so I hope the smell will last till midnight."

"What about me?" wailed Susan. "I haven't got anything! Mr Fox forced Asquith Minor to chuck my crucifix away!"

"You've got *us* to protect you," said Mr Fritz, reassuringly, though it was clear from Susan's face that this news didn't make much difference to her. "Now can you help me with this?"

His problem was to get six fat, dead flies glued into a very large catering-size coffee jar arranged so that there was a long line of them, right from the entrance of the jar to the bottom. "I've got a few more," he added, pointing to a paper bag. "I collected them from the cricket pavilion. We'll use those to lay a trail from Susan's windowsill."

"If we catch him, what do we do then?" asked Tom.

"*When* we catch him, not if," said Mr Fritz, rather tetchily. "*When* we catch him we'll throw him in the fire so he burns to death."

"Which fire?" asked Susan.

"Good point," said Mr Fritz looking round. "Oh, dear," he added, staring at one of the few empty spaces on the floor. "My firewood's gone! Mr Fox must have cleaned me out of that as well, because vampires hate fire. Oh well, there's nothing for it. It'll have to be my chair and a few of these old notes as kindling." He seized the chair from in front of his desk and started snapping off the legs one by one with a great crashing sound.

"Someone will hear us!" said Miles, worriedly. "Can't you do it quietly?"

"Now there's no way you can break up furniture quietly," explained Mr Fritz, patiently. "You see, the noise is created by the friction generated by the piece of wood splitting in two. This in turn creates noise or, as we call them, sound waves..."

"Yes, yes," said Miles, impatiently. "I'm sure that's right, but..."

"It *is* right, Miles," said Mr Fritz, slightly annoyed. "In the final analysis in science there's no room for thinking things might be so, or being almost certain they are so. They either are so or they aren't so. You must remember that or you'll never pass your GCSEs."

"At this rate we'll be lucky even to take them, let alone pass them," said Tom, gloomily.

"I'll remind you of that, when you're taking them, Tom," said Mr Fritz, with a twinkle in his eye. "I never thought I'd live to see the day I'd hear you saying you'd be *lucky* to take GCSEs!"

His jokes eased the tension and soon they were busy lighting the fire, rehearsing screwing on the lid of the coffee jar and planning how they would hide themselves in Susan's room.

By the time it got to 11.30 so many of the pupils were over-excited or exhausted there were sounds of wails, tears and hysterical giggles from the dormitories. The teachers seemed hyperactive, too, and as Mr Fritz and the children crept along the corridor to Susan's room, Tom clutching his Bible, they noticed a gaggle of them in Mr Carstairs' room, all cackling with laughter. Wild violin music floated out and they could see Signor Ruzzi standing on a chair playing an old gipsy fiddle; around him, in a crazy circle, danced the teachers, stamping and hooting like wild things.

"They've gone quite mad," whispered Miles. "Do you think they'll ever recover?"

Mr Fritz, who was hustling them along from behind, nodded. "Certainly. You see, they have not been subjected to the final rites. While they still eat earthly food – and it was clear from your mother's letter, Tom, that your father certainly had a good appetite – we know that they have not yet reached the stage of the last initiations. And certainly all the staff gobbled up their supper this evening. I suspect that Mr Culard is waiting to take his bride. Then and only then will he start his initiation rites."

Susan's side of the room was an utter mess. Old tights, pants, cans of hair spray and apple cores strewed the room. A broken typewriter lay in a corner on top of a pile of old folders and by her bed sat a half-eaten pot of strawberry jam with a spoon sticking out of it. It was a complete contrast to Rosemary's side, where ballet shoes were neatly arrayed along the floor, a tutu hung on the wall like a giant rosette and an enormous poster of Rudolph Nureyev beamed a toothy smile above the bed.

"It's worse than ours!" said Miles. "No wonder you don't let anyone in here. I thought it was your excessive sense of privacy but how wrong I was. You live in a pigsty!"

Susan glared at him, knowing she could hardly tell him to leave at a time like this. She seized Tom's Bible and stuck it near the window.

"That's to stop him getting in!" she said, triumphantly. But Mr Fritz strode over and took it back, opening the window and scattering a few dead flies outside as he did so.

"Susan, the idea is to lure him in, not keep him out," he said, crossly. "Now – the window's open. The lights should be kept on, but low. And perhaps you should sit at the window, Susan, preferably in your nightdress, combing your hair. So he can see you."

"I don't have a nightdress, thank you very much," said Susan. "I wear pyjamas! And I very rarely comb my hair."

Tom gave Miles a secret kick to stop him blurting out any more snide remarks.

"Well, we'll all go out and wait while you change," said Mr Fritz. "Come on, boys. No peeping, now."

They waited for about ten minutes outside the door listening to an angry clattering noise from Susan's room as she got changed. Then there was silence. Mr Fritz looked at his watch. It was nearly midnight. He waited another few minutes. Then: "Susan? Are you ready?" he whispered through the keyhole.

"Not quite," replied Susan. "Just a minute."

They waited five minutes longer. "Girls!" said Miles. "They take *hours* to change! I'd have got into my pyjamas in three seconds!"

Mr Fritz whispered through the door again. "Susan? Are you ready yet? We're getting worried."

"Don't come in for the moment," replied Susan. But her voice was different from normal. It was slurred and dull as if she were drunk.

In the corridor Miles and Tom looked at each other anxiously.

They waited another few minutes and finally Mr Fritz leant down and stared through the keyhole. Miles looked totally shocked and whispered: "Jeepers! What a dirty old man! Now I've seen everything!"

But Mr Fritz didn't hear him. He gave a sudden gasp. "Good heavens!" he whispered. "I think there's a bat in there. What fools we are! We should never have left her!"

Tom and Miles didn't hesitate for a moment. Tom grabbed the jar and they both burst in. Miles rushed over to shut the window with a crash.

"Here, take the Bible to stop him getting out!" cried Tom, throwing it over to Miles. He caught it and stood by the window, holding it in front of him like a shield. Mr Fritz stepped in quickly and shut the door behind him, putting his arms into the form of a cross.

Then they surveyed the scene.

Susan was sitting on the edge of her bed in her pyjamas, her head thrown back to expose as much of her slim, white neck as possible. A small, black bat fluttered round and round her head as if it were hypnotizing her, its wings making a rhythmic, flapping noise.

It gave a chirrup of rage when they came in, but that didn't stop its circling activities. Closer and closer it came to Susan's neck, each circle taking it nearer her soft, white skin. Tom, standing with the jar in his hand, felt his knees go weak. If it bit her, that would surely be the end. He could see its tiny teeth now, razor-sharp like ivory pins. They shimmered like two icy diamonds in its tiny, foul, hairy face. Between its teeth he could see an evil, pointed, red tongue, twitching excitedly.

Round and round went the bat, until Tom himself felt hypnotized.

"Chant your chant!" he whispered to Mr Fritz. "I feel I'm going under!"

"I can't remember it!" moaned Mr Fritz. "It's vanished from my mind. Count Dracula must have got all his powers going tonight. I can't even move!"

The bat continued fluttering, coming in closer and closer to Susan's neck and Susan herself gave a slight moan as if she were in a trance, leaning back even further. Then the bat, with a piping shriek of satisfaction, settled on her skin.

It was then that Tom felt the spell was broken. Mr Culard must have been concentrating so hard on getting his teeth into Susan's neck that he momentarily dropped his guard. Mr Fritz, also aware that Mr Culard's powers had relaxed, immediately remembered the words and started chanting: "In the name of the Lord! *Kanti, Kanti, el moranti, Jextapus sholem, vixit, vixit!*" Miles lunged forward with the Bible, breathing garlic breath in all directions, while Tom clamped the open jar onto Susan's neck, knocking her flying and, by smashing the jar onto the bedclothes, captured Mr Culard inside.

"Quick, quick, the top!" he shouted, and Miles pulled it out of his pocket. It was more difficult to screw the top on than they'd expected because to do so they had to lift the jar slightly from the bedclothes and risk Mr Culard escaping.

But Miles handed the top to Tom and breathed garlic all around the opening of the jar like a dragon, while Tom quickly whipped the jar upwards and screwed the top on as tightly as possible.

"The fire!" shouted Mr Fritz, grabbing the jar from Tom and rushing out of the room into the corridor.

Would they get there in time? Inside the glass jar, Mr Culard was going mad, crashing against the sides, hissing and squeaking. Mr Fritz looked down briefly and to his horror saw the bat slowly getting bigger and bigger. As he looked harder, he saw a small human ear growing out of the side of the bat's head. . .then the vestige of a hand pushing out from the wings. "My God, he's turning into Mr Culard!" he shouted, hurtling down the corridor to his room, with Miles and Tom chasing after him. "He'll soon break the jar!"

As he passed Signor Ruzzi's room, where the teachers had been singing and dancing earlier, six bats swooped out and battered against Mr Fritz's head, hissing and squawking, clawing at his eyes and face.

"Give it to me!" yelled Tom, haring up and catching the jar as Mr Fritz threw it to him. He raced off to Mr Fritz's room where the fire was roaring in a welcome blaze. As he threw the jar onto the fire, Mr Fritz followed, trying to tear the bats off his face, with Miles running close behind.

There was a vast explosion. The fire jumped and leapt and burst upwards as if a whole barrel of petrol had been poured onto the flames. From the fireplace came a sickening scream of pain and a cloud of acrid, green smoke poured into the room making them splutter and cough.

Susan staggered at the door in tears and Miles put his arm round her.

"Don't worry, everything's OK now," he said. "And you were absolutely marvellous."

"And so were you," said Susan, between sobs. "Both of you," she added as she saw Tom. "What would I have done without you? Jeepers, think of ending up as Mrs Culard! Can you imagine? I guess," she added, trying to summon up a rueful grin between her tears, "I'm just not cut out for marriage!"

As the smoke started to clear, Tom was aware of Mr Fritz in the corner, alternately coughing and shouting: "We've done it! We've defeated him! Thank the Lord!"

And then there was another voice joining in and Tom realized that the six bats had gone and in their place were the six teachers.

"Defeated who?" demanded Mr Fox, who was standing, confused, by the fire.

"Whom," corrected Mrs Grain, who was getting up from the floor. "It is the accusative and not the nominative."

"What a lovely, lovely fire!" cooed Miss Shepherd, moving forward, rubbing her hands. "I always think of flames as the sprites of Apollo, don't you?"

"But what are we doing here?" boomed Signor Ruzzi, rubbing his eyes. "I don't remember... I must have been asleep. And why, Mr Fritz, are you burning a skeleton on the fire might I ask? One of your leetle scientific experiments? But it makes a nasty smell, don't you theenk?"

"Skeleton, what skeleton?" asked Mr Fritz, as he pushed through the throng of teachers to stare into the grate. Good heavens, Signor Ruzzi was right. There, in the middle of the fire, was a grinning skull surrounded by ribs, hips and bits of spine. He shuddered.

"That's Mr Culard," he breathed. "How terrible."

"Mr who?" said Mr Fox coming closer to have a look. "Mr Culard? Who on earth is he?"

"The biology teacher," said Mr Fritz, "you know..."

"The biology teacher? Mr Culard? My dear old Fritz, are you all right? We have no biology teacher. Don't you remember...Cyril Cholmondely left at the beginning of the term and we've been without a teacher...or have we? My mind's playing funny tricks. But certainly I don't recall a Mr Culard."

"Nor do I," said Mrs Grain, scratching her head and then, surprised not to feel the familiar neat array of pins, she looked round for a mirror in Mr Fritz's room and finding none, stared at her reflection in the blackness of the window.

"What a fright I look!" she exclaimed. "What can have happened! I look as if I've just crawled from under a bush! What a dreadful example to set! I must tidy myself up." She sniffed. "Perhaps I should have a bath as well. Will the water still be hot?" She looked at her watch. "Mr Fox, it's 1.00 a.m.! We're up most awfully late! And what are you three doing here, might I ask?" she added, noticing Miles, Tom and Susan. "You should have been in bed hours ago!"

"Yes, we've got Wordsworth to study tomorrow," said Mr Carstairs, breezily. "Got to be up early in the morning to get to grips with Wordsworth, I always say. Fascinating character. And his *Prelude* is a truly *wonderful* evocation of a nineteenth century Lakeland childhood, full of passion and torment, yet with an underlying innocence that really gets you in the gut. Wordsworth, ah, Wordsworth, great mate of the poet Coleridge, you know, they were stoned the entire time. But on opium, that was what they liked. If they were alive today they'd probably be coking snort. Or whatever it is."

"But what about Dostoywhatsit's *Notes from the House of the Dead*?" piped up Tom. "I thought we were doing that for the last half of the term."

"Dostoywhatsit's – I mean Dostoevsky's *Notes from the House of the Dead*?" said Mr Carstairs in amazement. "What a dreadfully gloomy idea. I'd never suggest that."

"Well, come on, off to bed with you all. We've got to get up early for prayers tomorrow," said Mr Fox, yawning. "Thank you, Mr Fritz, for a most enjoyable evening round your fire. Have a good night's sleep. And God bless."

CHAPTER TWELVE

The last half of the term was refreshingly uneventful. Mr Roy returned to being a vegetarian, secretly wondering how on earth he could have choked down anything even as meaty as a tiny piece of cod; Miss Shepherd was transformed into her usual, fey self and no amount of holy flour sprinkled around her could provoke any reaction at all, except a breathless anxiety about how to clear it up; Mrs Grain got her bun into shape and stayed up all one night repairing her stockings, swiftly changing back into the dapper soul she used to be. Mr Carstairs continued his runs on his old route, leaping the stream with enthusiasm, and Signor Ruzzi's music cheered up no end, much to Mr Fox's sorrow who found Ruzzi's energetic and volatile spirits hard to take and secretly preferred his recent more funereal moods.

As for Mr Fox, he recovered completely. Like the rest of the teachers he could remember nothing at all of the events of the recent weeks – though he puzzled over a large order of bottled water and a weekly payment of twenty pounds that he was unable to account for. He couldn't have spent that much a week on alcohol, surely? He would have happily accused some of the staff of fiddling the books but he couldn't deny that these payments were written clearly in his own handwriting. Mr Fritz's behaviour had worried him recently – to have broken up his chair for firewood was surprising, not to mention burning skeletons in his grate. Mr Fox understood real skeletons to be rather pricey items – but no doubt Mr Fritz was simply carrying out one of his weird experiments. And there'd been no more trouble since he'd instructed Mr Fritz to help himself to a large pile of logs that had mysteriously appeared in one of the school out-houses.

To his amazement, when he discovered this cache of logs, he also found a whole stash of school mirrors along with several strings of garlic, school Bibles and prayer books. A funny kind of burglar he must have been, to steal and hide mirrors and garlic from the school – when he could have taken plenty of other more marketable commodities.

And how the devil had they coped for so long without a biology teacher? He only hoped that none of the children would mention this lack to their parents who would certainly be angling for refunds he could ill-afford. In a fit of panic he'd started teaching a spot of biology himself but couldn't remember for the life of him how one dissected a frog – or, indeed, distinguished a thorax from a stamen. Luckily he'd managed to contact an out-of-work supply teacher from Lanchester, a delightful woman who, it turned out, was the doctor's ex-wife. She seemed to have got every aspect of biology completely taped, not to mention the tricky topic of sex education which she was happy to dole out to all her classes. She even extended this service to Mr Fox – but in private of course.

Tom received a reassuring and affectionate letter from his dad apologizing for not writing and saying it was because he'd been ill. He explained that a couple of days ago, just past midnight, he'd suddenly woken up feeling absolutely marvellous and just like his old self. He also told him that Tom's grandmother had left them all her money which meant they'd be able to afford a holiday abroad next year for the first time. He had forgotten all about Mr Culard's visit.

Of Mr Culard himself there was no sign. Mr Fritz, Tom, Susan and Miles had sifted through the ashes in the grate but after the bat had turned into Mr Culard and then into a skeleton in the grate, nothing remained but a pile of grey dust and two blackened fangs.

"Hardly surprising, since he must have been some hundreds and hundreds of years old," said Mr Fritz, as he viewed the remains. "As you will know, the decomposition of bones takes place at a fairly rapid rate compared to say, stones. This is because bones are made up of calciferous substances. . ."

"Yes, yes," said Miles, totally uninterested. "But what about his coffin? Do you think that's still there?"

Mr Fritz clapped his hand over his mouth. "I forgot! Yes, we must check that just in case. . .we don't want any spare Transylvanian soil upsetting the balance of nature, do we?"

The coffin was indeed still in the wood with the lid upturned like an unmade bed, as if Mr Culard had only just climbed out. Mr Fritz had brought along some holy water that he'd filched from the font of the church after a recent christening and he sprinkled this over the coffin, saying a solemn prayer at the same time. There was a faint fizzing sound as the water touched the earth in the coffin, small columns of evil-smelling steam rose into the air and then, from the coffin's depths wriggled some fat, black worms which writhed painfully a few times and then expired with a disgusting pop.

Together they tipped the earth from the coffin, covered it with dead leaves and burnt it on top. The flames leapt high into the sky and as the coffin crackled into dust, Tom, Susan, Miles and Mr Fritz were all conscious of a tremendous relief.

"Well, that's that," said Miles, as they wandered back to the school for tea. "I must say I never want to look at a bat again in my life."

"Nor me," said Tom. "Though I suppose all that bat stuff might come in useful with exams. You never know."

"What are you two doing for Christmas?" asked Susan.

"I'm spending it in our castle in Scotland," said Miles. "I mean, *one* of our castles in Scotland."

"My Mom and Pop are taking me back to the States for Christmas," said Susan. "All the relations. Lots of turkey and pecan pie. How about you, Tom?"

"Oh, I'm just going home," said Tom, feeling warm inside at the thought. His own room, his hamster, his mum and dad, his friend Errol, the smell of fish and chips, the sound of the ice-cream van on the corner, his old black and white telly – soon to be exchanged for a colour one, according to his dad...all these things made it his own special home.

"Well, I'm returning to my friends in Romania for a typical Romanian Christmas," said Mr Fritz, rubbing his hands and smiling at the thought. "My woodcutter friend will undoubtedly be most impressed to hear of our success. And I hope you all have wonderful Christmases, too, by the way. You've been absolutely marvellous during all this. If it hadn't been for you, Count Dracula might have been well on his way to ruling the world. God bless you all."

"I'll go along with that," said Tom, remembering his mother's Bible with a smile. It had made a very useful bed-leg as well.

Miles put his hands together as if he were praying, pursed his lips, assumed a saintly expression and

175

chanted, "Aa-aa-men!"

"Awoman," muttered Susan.

And with that, they made their way over the darkening fields to tea.

THE KING AWAKES

Janice Elliott

Outcast from the City with his mother and baby sister young Red finds a Britain devastated by a nuclear holocaust and inhabited by savage tribes: Outmen, cannibals, Magickers and War Lords. Pursued by the evil Guardians, Red's one hope of survival lies with a mysterious stranger – a soldier woken from the distant past to fulfil a famous legend…

"An exciting tale of quest and pursuit." *The Listener*

The King Awakes is the first book in *The Sword and the Dream* triology. Look out for book two: *The Empty Throne*.

THE HORN OF MORTAL DANGER

Lawrence Leonard

When Jen and her brother Widgie stumble across a secret underground world, they find themselves in the middle of a war between two rival factions, the Railwaymen and Canal Folk. It is the start of a thrilling and dangerous adventure.

"A fantasy whose words are forcefully visual, whose concept is original and compelling."
Growing Point

"A lively, original and exciting adventure story."
The Times Literary Supplement